PIGGY™

AN ORIGINAL NOVEL

# PIGGY

## HUNT

by
**TERRANCE CRAWFORD**
and
**DAN WIDDOWSON**

Scholastic Inc.

This book is a work of fiction. Names, characters, places, and incidents are either
the product of the author's imagination or are used fictitiously, and any
resemblance to actual persons, living or dead, business establishments, events,
or locales is entirely coincidental.

ISBN 978-1-339-03943-5

10 9 8 7 6 5 4 3 2 1     24 25 26 27 28

Printed in the U.S.A.                40

First printing 2024

Book design by Jeff Shake

PIGGY HUNT

There had once been an island called Lucella. Far past Doveport and somewhere south of the North Sea, its outer edges were sprinkled with long beaches and stretches of picturesque mountains that led to a salting of dense forests. In the middle of the island was a city, a sprawling metropolis bustling with life. On a normal day, thousands of people went about their daily lives—searching for the perfect avocado at the grocery store or reading the paper on the Metro to work. On a normal day, crossing guards waved children across the street to school, and neighbors greeted one another cheerily as they passed one another on the streets. On a normal day, the sun hung low over the island, casting a lazy glow across the city. The island of Lucella had not had a normal day in quite some time.

If you were to ask those who were in the know, they would tell you that it had started off just like any other sickness. They would tell you that one day your neighbor would have a sniffle, or that your friend would have a cough that didn't sound quite right. By the time the fevers started, it was too late. The people of Lucella were going to sleep and waking up as something . . .

not quite themselves. Their eyes were beginning to glow, their walks stiffened to a lumbering gait, and they were beginning to smell like the worst part of a hot summer day. Whatever the sickness was, it had turned normal, everyday people into grisly, gruesome, ghoulish shadows of their former selves.

"Hold it down!" Ben shouted as loudly as he could muster, struggling to be heard over the loud, unpleasant, and prolonged sounds the infected creature was making. The thing thrashed wildly in Ben's grasp, squealing loudly as it tried to break free. It may not

have looked like it—fist balled tightly around the creature's tattered shirt, and a cure-loaded quick-release syringe poised to go in his outstretched hand—but Ben was trying to help. The creature wriggled its body once more, this time its haphazard movements accompanied by a terrifying scream. Ben held the creature in place as best he could, but coming in direct contact with the teeth or claws of the Infected was as good as asking for the Infection.

Ben narrowly dodged a swipe from the massive creature's untrimmed cloven hoof; the syringe holding the cure was not lucky enough to share that same fate. The creature knocked the vial out of Ben's hand, and Ben's eyes followed it as it twisted in the air, end over end, before finally landing in the grass a few yards from where the two sat. The creature noticed as well, taking advantage of the momentary chaos and confusion to roughly tackle Ben to the ground. The two opposing forces tussled some more in the dirt, neither gaining the upper hand for longer than a couple of moments. In any given person's life, there are three, maybe four moments that cause one to truly stop and reflect on the

choices that led them to said moment. Rolling around in the dirt, trying to restrain something nearly twice his size so that he could administer a glowing blue cure created by the military in a supersecret lab up North, was the first of those moments in Ben's young life.

These past several months had been both long and eventful, to say the least. Ben remembered how things used to be. He remembered when he would count down the days until summer vacation. Three whole months of no school, no bedtime, and all the online survival horror-based video games that he could handle. This summer, Ben was simply grateful for the few extra hours of sunlight keeping at bay the sea of glowing red eyes that seemed to follow him and his friends wherever they went. It had been a crisp autumn day when Ben had left his home, not knowing then that he was taking the first steps in what would become the adventure of a lifetime. Back then, the dense, nearly solid layer of fog that enshrouded the city seemed almost seasonally appropriate, before it had become a seemingly permanent fixture of the landscape of Lucella.

Now, with Ben spending each day out in the elements, every day was either too hot or too cold. On the days that the sun managed to fight its way through the haze of cloud cover, Ben found it entirely too hot, salt constantly stinging his eyes as he wiped sweat from his brow. Most days, however, Ben and his friends were at the mercy of the almost supernatural chill that hung in the air over the island, no matter the actual temperature. Seasons had come and gone, days turning into weeks and weeks turning into months, but the chill lingered. It was little to no wonder that Ben still clung so preciously to the hooded black leather jacket he had been wearing since the beginning of this adventure. Of course, the elements were not the only thing from which Ben was seeking protection.

Ben had been aware of the Infection from the beginning. At first, even if no one you knew had caught it, it was impossible to escape the specter that the news cast over Lucella—the hushed whispers on street corners, the three-minute bits on the early evening news, the news ticker that scrolled by beneath every television program. Awareness was all well and good, but nothing prepared you for seeing one of the things up close and in person.

The first time Ben had seen one of the creatures was at the home of his best friend, Ollie. One may not have been able to figure it out by looking at him, but the young man currently pinned to the ground by a quarter of a ton of breathing abomination had not set out to be some kind of postapocalyptic war hero. Before this had all begun—before the cure vials, before the police station, and long before the giant killer spiders—Ben had been on a simple mission to find his friend. That one objective had been the driving force behind everything that had happened to Ben over the last several months.

Of course, Ollie was not to blame. It was hard enough to let your friends and family know where to find you these days, even more so if you weren't certain if there was anyone around to look for you. To his credit, in the time that Ben had been looking for his lost friend, Ollie had become quite adept at looking out for himself. All that time surviving alone among the elements had hardened his exterior, if not his personality.

If Ben had to take a guess, he would have wagered that Ollie had more experience fighting off the Infected than even Ben, and at this point, that was no small feat. Ben had been up against more than his fair share of the things. He shuddered as he remembered the mysterious Mr. P—a disembodied voice who seemed to exist only on the other side of his walkie-talkie. Ben had been flipping through the channels on his walkie-talkie one evening when he had heard the man's pleas for help. Ben had rescued the man's missing friend, Bunny, and she in turn had rescued him.

Ben had heard rumors floating around The Safe Place that Mr. P was a millionaire or that he owned a helicopter, but the truth was, no one knew for sure. Ben and Ollie's eventual reunion had been interrupted by the arrival of a swarm of the Infected, not surprising to absolutely anyone who possessed the ability to recognize patterns. The duo had been pinned against a wall, trapped by a sea of glowing red eyes. What had once been a terrifying harbinger of doom was now an all too familiar everyday sight. The only thing that had saved Ben's and Ollie's respective skins from the bloodthirsty crowd of ghouls had been the timely and somewhat dramatic arrival of Billy and Badgy, agents of The Silver Paw.

As it turned out, Ben and Ollie weren't the only survivors. Dozens of people had banded together under the leadership of a wolf named Willow and formed a militia of sorts, based at The Safe Place. Billy was a gentle giant, a massive bull who was also the friendliest person Ben had ever met. Everything a person could ever want to know about Billy could be explained by the weapon he had chosen to wield against the end of the world: a stainless-steel barbell with a pair of weighted plates on either side. Badgy was a badger, and Billy's constant companion. If he thought about it, Ben wasn't sure if he had ever seen the two apart. Although Badgy was admittedly not as friendly as Billy, Ben liked to think that he had peeled back Badgy's gruff exterior and gotten to know his prickly, gruff interior as the quartet had journeyed to and from—and then back to—The Safe Place.

The Safe Place—the most aptly named point on the island—was a five-story building in the heart of the city of Lucella. The exterior was cold and gray, projecting a facade so seemingly impenetrable that you would never know that just beyond the thrice-bolted double doors lie five storage rooms, a laundry room, a gym, a cafeteria, a main room, a radio room, and enough bedrooms to accommodate the displaced of Lucella.

Ben had not spent as much time as he would have liked at The Safe Place; he had barely had enough time to verify that his parents were safe and accounted for before he was being hustled into a single room in the basement, whiteboards and computers spread across every inch of available wall space. Willow had a mission for him, and she did not seem like the type of wolf to take "no" for an answer. There were rumors, whispered on the wind from survivors from across the island, that there was a way to fix the people who had been turned wild by the Infection. They were calling it a cure. Less than twenty-four hours after Willow had received the intel, Ben and Ollie had been dispatched to go investigate, Billy and Badgy in tow. It was a journey that had taken them from the once-bustling metropolis of the city of Lucella to the massive tree-laden forests just outside town, the quartet picking up components of the purported cure everywhere they went. Their journey eventually brought them to a place called Doveport, a city across the North Sea. According to the research journals from the old military base, this is where the traveling group of adventurers would find the final components of the cure.

Lucella boasted a slight chill in the air and a seemingly never-ending supply of fog that had accompanied the arrival of the virus, but it was still better than the nearly solid sheet of snow that blanketed Doveport at all times. Both were probably results of weather patterns from being so close to the North Sea, but only one managed to soak through Ben's jacket and chill him to the bone. What the group had thought to be the final piece of the cure was hidden deep underground, stashed away deep in the cavernous tunnels that snaked beneath the massive stone temple in Doveport.

Of course, true to form, that was not the only thing that lay beneath the temple. Ben and his companions had to dodge giant axes swinging from the ceiling and solve a series of wheel puzzles to gain access to the underground passageways, and they still had not faced the deadliest part of their journey. That came in the form of a creature called Spidella, a hulking and heavily built infected creature with eight legs and no compunctions about trapping her hapless victims in her web and doing what giant spiders were wont to do. Ben had seen some incredible, horrible things since the Infection had come to settle in Lucella, but all of them paled in comparison to Spidella. Twice Ben's size and at least as heavy, Spidella was a nightmare creature with eight elephantine legs, four beady black eyes, and small, needlelike hairs all over her massive abdomen.

Navigating the labyrinthine tunnels beneath the temple had been scary enough, to say nothing of being pursued by a giant spider. Ben and his companions had found the final ingredient of the cure, and not a moment too soon. Ollie had fallen prey to one of Spidella's webs, and the Infection was already beginning to spread. It was thanks only to the labs beneath the temple, Ben's quick acting, and the radioactive tubing that Badgy had been using as a weapon that they were able to fashion a rudimentary version of the cure and save Ollie from the same grisly fate that had befallen much of his hometown.

Ben was relieved to discover that he found the journey up through the caverns much simpler than the journey down, having been largely relieved of the pressure of being chased by an eight-legged monster. Lucky for the fearless adventurers, they reached the docks of Doveport without any further incidents with the Infected. Billy was more than strong enough to push an unclaimed boat from the

North Docks into the sea with everyone aboard, and it turned out that Badgy was even a half-decent navigator when he wasn't murmuring angrily under his breath about the weather. Ollie had started feeling better almost immediately, the cure working rapidly to reverse the effects of Ollie's brief infection, much to Ben's relief.

A few more days' trek had led them back to the rigid familiarity and bright fluorescent lighting of The Safe Place. Willow had of course wanted a rundown of everything that had occurred in their search for the cure. The best and brightest minds available to them had pored over every note that Ben had found regarding the cure, and there were weeks of testing and experiments until one day, the experts announced that they had finally done it and the cure was ready for distribution. Of course, someone still had to go out and administer the cure. That, it seemed, was where Ben and his friends came in.

A loud screech from the infected creature in front of him snapped Ben out of his reverie and away from a very thorough and well-explained recap.

"Hold him down!" Ben repeated, hoping that his friends could hear him over the ear-splitting screams of the Infected.

"I'm trying!" came Ollie's reply from the other side of the creature, voice trembling as the creature tried in vain to shake Ollie off its leg. "Badgy! We could really use some help over here!"

Ø Ø Ø

"Are you kidding me? I'm not touching that thing, look at it!" Badgy shouted back, raising a crossbow to the level of his eye. Badgy was right—the infected creatures were truly a sight to behold. Their clothes were tattered from weeks' and weeks' worth of use, their lifeless eyes now mismatched red and black, and the sight of uninfected people made them drool—literally. It was not work for the weak of stomach. "Besides, I work better from a distance."

Ben certainly couldn't begrudge Badgy his distance. The white badger had been more hesitant to jump into the muck of it all since he had lost the weapon that he had been using since Ben had met him, a glowing, green, radioactive container currently being used as part of the cure. The very same cure that filled the darts of Badgy's new crossbow. Badgy moved the bow back and forth, trying to get a solid lock on the creature. It was hard enough trying to cure an epidemic of infected ghouls with a tool from before the Common Era; even more so when your target was wrestling with your team on the ground.

## THUNK THUNK!

Badgy's aim and train of thought were interrupted by the loud clanking sound of metal hitting earth. A monstrous figure loomed over Ben and Ollie, casting a dark shadow that blocked out the sun. Ben took a deep breath, the creature he had been trying to hold down now pinned to the ground with a metal bar. Raising his hand to the level of his eyes, he let out a sigh of relief. "Billy!" Ollie let out a relieved chuckle as well, scampering quickly away from the still screeching creature.

"Were you expecting the *Tooth Fairy*?" replied their quite literally bullish friend. He extended his hand, yanking Ollie's slight frame off the ground as he lifted him to his feet.

"Okay—not to be the guy who spouts cliché post-action dialogue," Ollie said between staggered attempts to catch his breath, brushing dirt and grass from his pants and shirt and wiping sweat from his brow, "but that was close."

Billy nodded, beaming with pride as a goofy grin graced his bovine features. "What would you guys do without me?"

Badgy made his way to the group, abandoning the higher ground and vantage point of the hill across the way. "You mean, what would we do first?" The cranky badger loaded a cure capsule into his crossbow, pulling the mechanism back and launching the dart at the pinned creature. "I'm thinking a party. Maybe some cake, sparkling grape juice, maybe a big banner that says—"

The creature squealed loudly as the cure began to take effect, cutting off what was sure to be a serious contender for the most sarcastic thing that Ben had ever

heard. Its black eyes rolled back into its head, unclouding and revealing a pair of bright blue irises. The creature's gaze darted around the hill—taking in two children, a badger, and a bull—before flitting shut, sleep overtaking him. That was how it usually went. The formerly infected creature would wake up with a splitting headache, but without the intense and all-consuming desire to attack their friends and loved ones. A pretty fair trade as far as Ben was concerned.

Billy reached down and grabbed his barbell, the now formerly Infected snoring heavily, sleeping off what must have been weeks of ghoulish behavior.

Muffled static crackled, a familiar voice filtering through tinny speakers. "Blue Team? Blue Team, come in. Over."

If Ben thought that Willow—the leader of The Silver Paw and their team's liaison at The Safe Place— sounded severe in person, her voice filtering through the walkie-talkie was certainly not doing her any favors. Ben's backpack was nearby, having been discarded in favor of a more stealthy approach, a strategy that had ended with Ben on his back and one of the creatures bearing down upon him. Needless to say, it was a tactical mistake he would not make again. He rummaged around in his nearby discarded pack for the walkie-talkie, flipping the small plastic device open and holding down the transmission button. "Gold Team, this is Blue Team, we read you loud and clear." There was a heavy silence on the other end, as if Willow was waiting for something. Ben sighed, rolling his eyes as he lifted the wallow-talkie back to his mouth. "Over."

Static crackled on the other end of the line as Willow spoke. "Status report, Blue Team. Over."

Ben took a quick look around, assessing the terrain. The quartet of adventurers didn't seem to be in any immediate danger, and Ben had gotten quite good at discerning danger. "Uhh, situation normal, Gold Team. We just distributed another dose of the cure, and the subject is sleeping like a baby. Uhh, pretty standard stuff. Over."

"What did you expect, boss?" chimed Badgy's scratchy baritone from the background. "You sent in *professionals*." Another heavy silence. "And I'm not saying 'over'!" Badgy added.

Static sounded once again from the other end of the line. "So no incidents that I should be aware of? No one on your team almost got stepped on? Over," Willow inquired over the walkie-talkie. Ben swallowed dryly, looking around at his friends. Willow was the head of the Lucella militia and very good at her job, which meant that she had eyes and ears all over the island, but she couldn't have eyes and ears *all* over the island, could she?

Ben raised the walkie-talkie back to his mouth, clearing his throat before he spoke. "No, uh . . . everything is good here. Why do you ask?"

This time, the response from the other end came almost instantly. "You *professionals* left your walkie-talkie channel open. We can hear everything that's going on. Over."

Ben frantically rotated the plastic device in his hand, turning it end over end to locate the transmission button. The walkie-talkie had been gifted to him by a police officer and had been with him on most of his journey since. It was still largely functional, even if it had seen better days. Sure enough, the switch that held open the channel to The Safe Place was locked in place, broadcasting their every word back to the Lucella stronghold. It must have come undone during his impromptu wrestling match with the infected creature. Ben grimaced, thankful at the very least that Willow could not see the embarrassment on his face. "Ah. Okay, well the thing about that is—I can explain . . ."

"Never mind that," Willow interrupted. "We need you back at The Safe Place. There has been a development." Ben raised an eyebrow at her choice of words. Coming from Willow, "developments" were almost never good. Never had a development developed into a weeklong vacation or a new soft-serve machine in The Safe Place cafeteria, instead almost always having to do with another den of Infected that needed clearing. Ben repressed a loud sigh, raising the device back to his face.

"Over and out" came Willow's voice through the box, the signal cutting out abruptly before Ben could have a chance to argue. Ben clicked the walkie-talkie off, double-checking the device before tossing it into his backpack and hoisting the carryall onto his back and tightening the straps around his shoulders. He looked around at his friends, all looking to him for direction. "Well, fellas. You heard the wolf. We're going home."

PIGGY HUNT

The trek to the nearest Metro station did not take the quartet of adventurers long. Like any major city worth its salt, Lucella had invested heavily in public transit. The trains had long since been automated, which meant that they came both frequently and on time. The fearless foursome traipsed quickly down the stairs into the Metro station, the foggy, overcast skies of Lucella giving way to the dim, buzzing overhead lights of the subway. Ben and Ollie ducked underneath the turnstiles that barred entry to the station while Badgy hopped over them, opening the emergency door for Billy, whose massive size almost guaranteed that he could not use the regular entrance. An alarm rang lazily, almost to no one in particular. Fare evasion was a crime, but a boundlessly cool one with no real victims and whose consequences there was no one around to enforce.

Ben felt his shoulders drop, relaxing just a little bit as they entered the underground station. Over the course of his adventures, Ben had become no stranger to roaming the island of Lucella on foot, but now that they had a cure for the illness, reliable transportation had quickly become paramount to their needs. This meant that the half dozen or so Metro stations peppered across the island had been the first locations cleared out by Ben, his friends, and the combined might of The Silver Paw.

Ben looked overhead at the dimly illuminated sign that displayed the upcoming subway's arrivals and departures. According to this train schedule, the next train they could take to The Safe Place would be there in fewer than five minutes. Ben took a seat; the rigid wooden benches provided by the Metro station were not intended for comfort or relief, instead seemingly only there by requirement. The laminated wood had begun to splinter and crack from months without upkeep and pieces of the bench jutted out at weird angles, ostensibly to keep people from using them as a place to sleep. Ben kicked his feet up, anyway, stretching his tired legs across the seats, his eyes drifting closed, and he rested his head against the beige tile wall of the station. He had learned a great deal of things since he had first set out on this journey, an important one being to rest when he could.

He very rarely got the opportunity, and so it would take more than a little hostile architecture to keep him from catching a few minutes' peace.

Not *much* more, however, Ben discovered as a horrible smell tickled his nostrils, dragging his half-awake brain kicking and screaming back to the land of consciousness. His eyes shot open as he heard the familiar click of Badgy loading a fresh vial of the cure into his crossbow, the bad-tempered badger aiming down the sights of his weapon at a single solitary glowing red eye in the near distance. Ben scrambled to his feet, his already sore legs practically screaming for a break as his hands flew to his hip and the small, handheld electroshock taser that he had kept on his person since it had been given to him.

The red-eyed creature lurched forward, the buzzing and crackling overhead fluorescents exposing the creature to the light. Ben had seen his fair share of these monsters and if he never saw another, it would be far too soon, but never had that been more true than in this moment. While most of the infected creatures that the group came across were horrid in both smell and appearance, this one raised the bar in the most odious of ways.

The infected creature towered over everyone except Billy, taking labored and rasping breaths as it stumbled toward the quartet on legs as thick as tree trunks. Black veins sprouted like plant roots from behind the thing's eyes, spreading across its face. Whereas every creature they had run afoul of to this point had boasted the same dull pink skin, this one looked even more sickly, the overhead lights casting dancing, flickering shadows across the creature's sunken, sagging, sallow skin.

The ghoulish beast's jaw went slack as it took another slow, measured step toward the heroes of Lucella, exposing a mouth filled with teeth the shape of tombstones, each a different size and color—none of them looking as if they had seen recent dentistry work. One of its eyes bulged from its head, glowing a sickly orange-and-red color, in a way that was equal parts frightening and hauntingly familiar. The dark veins blotting its face resumed on its arms, ending in twisted and decrepit limbs the color of black licorice, limbs that seemed to have long since abandoned the idea of being attached to a living being.

Ben tried breathing through his mouth to abate the smell, but it was to no avail. He had been able to get through the smell of the Infected before—sometimes he hardly even noticed it anymore—but this was almost a solid, like wading through a stench with the consistency of pudding or being force-fed old waffle batter off your grandfather's favorite coat. Characteristically, Badgy was the one to break the silence.

"Buddy, you smell like c—"

"Decay!" Ben shouted, throwing out the first word that came to mind in an effort to protect Ollie's young, innocent ears. His friends turned to him, confused by his outburst, but keeping their eyes trained on the monster in front of them.

"Yeah, well, I don't know who DK is," Ollie piped up, "but this guy is really going through it."

"The train is coming . . ." Billy warned, teetering back

and forth on his hooves, his dumbbell rod raised over his head in anticipation of battle. "Maybe you should cure this sucker; the next train isn't for another ten minutes."

"What? You got somewhere to be?" Badgy asked sarcastically.

"Does a bull go in the woods?" Billy replied. "No, he doesn't. Because that's not gentlemanly, so yeah. I'd like to make this train!"

Badgy pulled back the string on his crossbow, locking the mechanism into place as he aimed through the circular scope affixed to the stock of the device.

"Nighty night . . ." Badgy whispered through gritted teeth as the retention spring shot forward, launching a syringe of the cure at the creature called DK. The vial went wide, bouncing off the ceiling before shattering on the ground behind DK. The group's eyes widened in horror and shock, each coming to rest back on Badgy.

"You . . . missed?!" Ollie shouted, putting words to what everyone else was thinking.

"It's not as easy as moving and clicking a mouse, you know!" Billy threw up his massive hands in exasperation, drawing a sharp glare from his old companion. "Hey! These things take a lot of practice, and in case you ain't noticed . . ." Badgy threw up his own hand to mirror Billy's. "I ain't exactly got the best hand-eye coordination do I?"

Badgy took another vial of the cure from the clip around his waist, loading it into his crossbow and firing again. This shot landed true, striking DK directly in its shoulder. The plunger activated, pumping the glowing blue liquid directly into the massive creature's body. In just a few moments from now, the brutish creature would be on the ground, dreaming the deepest of dreams. Seconds that felt like minutes passed, the ghoulish figure in front of them showing no signs of weariness. Four pair of eyes darted back and forth between one another, all ostensibly thinking the same thing. *It didn't usually take this long, did it?*

Finally, the creature moved. Raising a bedraggled arm to the syringe plunged into its shoulder, it curled long

spindly fingers around the vial and pulled it out. Even Ben, rooted to the ground in fear, took a step back. He had seen Badgy take this same shot a dozen times. This same dosage had felled lions and tigers and—if Ben's memory was not failing him, even a few bears. Oh, my. The distorted monster dropped the container on the ground in front of it, crushing it under a giant foot. The monster took another rasping breath.

"Don't."

Ben's blood ran cold. He had seen the infected people of Lucella do incredible things over the last couple of months. He had seen them tear through buildings like they were made of cardboard and he had seen them throw full-grown Silver Paw agents across the room like they were children's toys. He had never heard one of the creatures speak.

"That's new, right?" Ollie asked. "That's new to the canon?" Ben felt the blood rush to his ears and his knees go weak. Time slowed to a crawl. A low rattling sound filled the air, signaling the arrival of the train. The subway rumbled into the tunnel, bathing everyone in its light. Call it intuition, call it instinct, call it guts—call it whatever you wanted, but everything in Ben's body was screaming at him to run. Rooted to the ground in horror, Ben finally convinced his legs to listen to his brain. Ben began to step backward, not taking his eyes off the distorted creature in front of him. Ollie, Billy, and Badgy took his cue, each turning tail to run back to the end of the Metro station tunnel. The train made an abrupt, lurching stop, steel-colored doors sliding open with a dull whooshing sound.

"STAND CLEAR OF THE DOORS" came a garbled automated voice from over the tinny speakers. The four hustled back into the corner of the train, though the distorted monster DK hadn't so much as blinked since it had spoken. The doors to the train whisked shut and the train rumbled to life, wobbling forward along the track. Ben looked back through the scratched plexi-glass window of the train, the monstrous creature fading into the nothingness of the dark Metro station tunnel, a glowing red orb growing smaller and smaller as the train rolled along the tracks. Ben's legs finally caught up with him and buckled, and he collapsed onto the cold plastic seat of the train, burying his head in his hands. A thousand questions raced through his mind. Had the original Infection mutated? Was this new strain resistant to the cure that they had only just discovered? Since when did the infected creatures talk? Though the one question that rang loudest in his mind—

"What was *that*?" Badgy shouted, his scratchy voice echoing throughout the empty subway car as he gave voice to what everyone else was thinking. "That wasn't no regular ghoul back there; what was that?" The silence that followed Badgy's manic

32

query seemed to be the best answer that anyone could give him.

Eventually, the adrenaline from their unorthodox encounter began to wear off. Billy fell victim to the lure of sleep first, his head laying heavily on the backpack Ben had taken from Officer Doggy all that time ago. Billy's chest heaved in and out slowly as he snored deeply, seemingly too deep in slumber to hear the loud metal clanking of his barbell as it rattled along the train car floor. Ollie yawned, stretching his arms over his head. It was not long before he, too, was fast asleep, his head propped up on one of Billy's massive legs. Even Badgy stopped pacing the length of the subway car, muttering under his breath, and took a seat on one of the rigid plastic benches—still muttering under his breath. Ben held a hand over his chest, his heart still pounding and his breaths still coming in rapid bursts. He took a few steady, measured breaths, trying to get his breathing under control. With each breath, Ben relaxed a little, feeling his blocky shoulders drop. His eyelids fluttered and closed as he drifted off to sleep.

Ben could not remember the last time he had gotten a proper good night's sleep. Maybe it had been that first night in the forest with Officer Doggy, but if that's the bar he was setting for himself, it was a low one to clear indeed. Tonight would not be that night. After their encounter with the distorted monster in the Metro station lobby, Ben wasn't exactly surprised.

As the rhythmic rocking motion of the underground train lulled Ben to sleep, he found himself back on the train platform, the ghastly distorted monster standing before him just as it had not hours ago. Ben looked around—Ollie, Badgy, and Billy were nowhere to be found. In his hands, Ben held Badgy's crossbow, a set of three cure-loaded crossbolts inlaid into the device. Ben triggered the firing mechanism, the first of the cure vials launching in slow motion until it landed squarely in the creature's chest. The syringe plunger activated and the monstrous creature fell down at Ben's feet. The version of Ben in his dream edged closer and closer to the unconscious creature until he stood over it, looking down into its mismatched eyes. Gravity shifted and Ben fell, the creature's eyes widening to swallow his whole body. He landed softly in an empty room, bathed entirely in the same eerie crimson glow that emanated from the eyes of the Infected. Ben's eyes scanned his surroundings frantically, settling on a figure in black looming ever larger in the distance. The Entity turned toward Ben and he jolted in his sleep as he felt a pang of recognition wash over him. Ben had hit several significant growth spurts over the summer, like many kids his age, but the Entity still towered over him, casting a literal shadow over Ben as he moved

toward him. This was not the first time Ben had dreamed of this man, and he wasn't alone.

Several residents of The Safe Place had reported seeing the same man in their dreams, each time spreading spite and whispering wickedness. No one knew who he truly was, only that he was effectively the boogeyman of Lucella. The Entity appeared to people in their dreams when they were feeling low or when they were feeling vulnerable, and he tried to manipulate them to his own nefarious ends. Just what were those nefarious ends? Well, that remained to be seen. There was no mistaking the specter before Ben. His face was an uneven patchwork of gray stitching and skin the texture of a burlap potato sack with a button-shaped patch over one eye. The eye left exposed was large and gave off a reddish-orange glow as it bulged from the right side of his face.

Ben felt the bottom fall out from his stomach when he realized why the distorted monster from the Metro station's platform had looked so familiar to him. He had seen the very same eye looking at him once before. The man stood out against the ghoulish crimson background of the dream, his dark purple blazer folded smartly over a light purple shirt with three gleaming black buttons. A red bow tie fit smartly around his neck, lanky, slender legs and feet filled out a pair of purple pants and black shoes, and white gloves covered spindly fingers. A purple top hat sat upon the Entity's head as if to complete his look, a long piece of black trim running along the bottom of the hat and encircling the middle. Pinning together this milliner's worst nightmare was a flower—a midnight black stamen that blossomed into a ring of orange petals. The petals had begun to die off, the withering plant beginning to blacken and curl at the ends, making the flower heavily resemble the eyes of the Entity and the distorted monster from the Metro station platform. There were rumors that he had even inspired a following—a motley crew of outsiders and wackadoos who knelt at the altar of his creepiness. If the whispers floating around The Safe Place were to be believed, and they often were, the group was using this symbol as a calling card: a single black orb followed by a ring of crimson, then encircled again by a ring of black. They were calling it "the Eye of Insolence," because of course they were.

Ben turned to face the fearsome being before him. Ben had heard him called a great many names. Some called him the Insolent One, with fear ringing every syllable of the name as they spoke. Ben preferred the "Entity," a name he had heard from one of the adults at The Safe Place—it expressed a dearth of knowledge about the man's origins without leaning into the fear that he so clearly craved. Ben had not been to his history class in quite some time now, but if his memory was correct, those who tried to rule through fear were often not looked back upon too fondly.

Some skipped the pleasantries altogether and called the man the Iniquitous One. A white gloved finger curled and uncurled, beckoning Ben forward. In the realm of his dreams, Ben was not in full control of his body, so he did as the Entity commanded, the distance between the two closing rapidly as Ben seemed to glide across the scarlet floor to the besuited nightmare man. He came to an abrupt halt in front of the Entity, that horrible glowing eye looking him over, probing for any sort of weakness or vulnerability that it could exploit. Finally, the Inquitous One opened his mouth to speak.

"I've been . . . fascinated by you for quite a while." The Entity spoke slowly and deliberately, his voice like nails on a chalkboard echoing through Ben's head. No, not fingernails—the kind you would find at a hardware store. "You're unique, Ben."

Ben wanted to argue but found no words leaving his mouth. He wasn't unique; he was just a young man in an open-world platform. The Entity seemed to sense Ben's apprehension.

"Ah, don't be modest, young man. You're extraordinary, and you're not like the others." What did the Iniquitous One mean by that? Again, the mysterious figure before him answered his question before he could ask it. "You're supposed to be infected. Do you remember when your journey began, Ben? Before the police station. Before the forest. Before the grocery store and all the labs. Think, Ben. *Think*."

The first place that Ben had explored in his search for Ollie was his friend's home. He remembered it like it had happened this morning as opposed to months and months ago. He remembered that it was the first time he had seen one of the Infected. It had attacked him in a frenzy; what was now par for the course at the time seemed like a novel way to perish. He had narrowly avoided the thing, using his friend's house keys to lock the creature inside the empty house. Ben had been, for the first time but not the last, lucky. He had managed to survive that encounter, coming out with nothing but a small scratch from the infected creature's hooves.

"There it is." The Entity's voice broke through Ben's memory. "But you're not. You're alive. You're . . ." The Entity's voice trailed off, leaving Ben to complete the train of thought for himself. Ben had been facing the elements and the infected creatures for months now, and he had not so much as broken a fever. But there was no way that the Entity could know any of that. Even Willow and her agents at The Silver Paw didn't know the details of Ben's adventures before he had come to them, and Willow was proud of saying that she had "eyes and ears all over the island" to any lower-ranking Silver Paw agent that she could harangue into listening to her. Though perhaps she wasn't the only one. As Ben thought back over his journey, he remembered every time that he had felt a pair of eyes on him from a distance—a horrible red orb floating just out of reach, watching him without him knowing.

The Entity nodded his head slowly as Ben came to the realization that he was being guided to, an upturned smile on the Entity's face making him look all the more unsettling. "Don't you see? You're immune to the Infection. You have much potential to do things beyond your understanding." Ben urged himself to wake up, to no avail. The nightmare continued. He had no desire to join the man who came to people in their dreams and whispered wickedness into their ears. All Ben wanted was for things to go back to normal, but truthfully, he wasn't quite sure what that would even look like anymore.

"I can help you see your friends again," the Entity said, waving his white-gloved hands in the air. A half-dozen figures began to glide forth from the shadows, lining up in front of the Iniquitous One as he presented them to Ben, his face pulled up at the corners by a smile like an anglerfish. Ben would recognize the brown snout and blue police uniform of Officer Doggy anywhere, even in a dream. He had lost the canine officer in the forest. They had managed to drive from the police station to the art gallery, fighting off the Infected all the way, but after they made their way into the forest that bordered the main city of Lucella . . . Officer Doggy had simply disappeared, literally overnight. Ben had always hoped that he had gotten somewhere safe.

The next figure revealed himself as Badgy, his right arm glowing a bright green color, holding his old radioactive container. The glow from his arm and the container shone a light on the other figures—Ollie, Billy, and Sally Squirrel. Ben's eyes widened as he took her in, those same dark eyes, pink nose, and ever-twitching ears. Sally was a friend of Mr. P's, the voice on the other end of Officer Doggy's radio. She had been hiding from the infected creatures in the base-ment of the school when Ben had been tasked with rescuing her, and together they had fought their way out the building. The two had made it to the downtown Metro station, but that was where they had been overtaken, overwhelmed, and cornered by a swarm of the massive, mutated monsters. Sally had given herself up to the creatures to keep them at bay, attempting to fend off a veritable horde of monsters with nothing but an old crossbow and a handful of carrots. The last time he had seen her had been from the back of a subway train car, shrinking into the distance against a sea of monsters. If she had not been so brave, Ben's journey might have come to a much more sudden and grisly end.

"I can help you see them all again . . ." the Entity repeated. "You are a strong, resilient, and talented warrior. There is much you can do for me in return."

Ben considered the offer for a moment, mulling it over in his head. On the one hand, he very badly wanted to know what had happened to his friends. The last time he had seen Sally Squirrel and Officer Doggy had been in less than ideal situations, and Ben had not realized how much he missed them both until their shadowy facsimiles had appeared before him. On the other hand, Ben had seen some truly horrifying things over the past several months, and somehow, the Entity was worse than all of them. The Insolent made his blood run cold and the pit drop out from the bottom of his stomach. Ben knew his answer. It seemed that the two did not have a deal. The Entity's wide, stringed smile contorted in dismay, eyes bulging with barely contained rage bubbling just beneath the surface.

"Are you rejecting my offer?" the Entity questioned, his voice tinged with anger. The Entity's face dropped. Gone now was any facade of goodness from the Entity. All false affectations of benevolence seemed to disappear the moment that Ben had rejected the Inquitous One's offer.

"Hm. So be it." The Entity's voice boomed, almost filling the room. "They're always stubborn at first. Then, when they have no one left, they come right back to me."

The Entity took a step forward, cackling maniacally as he began to grow, doubling and tripling in size before Ben's very eyes, until the Entity stood towering over him. His features stretched, becoming more distorted and grotesque, his legs shrinking into his body and his fingers growing long, sharp talons. The smart and stylish suit he had been wearing melted into a puddle of black sludge that covered the Entity's entire body, contrasted only by a white, glowing heart in the center of his form and the crimson bow tie still wrapped around his neck. Holes appeared all over and throughout the Entity's body, the redness of their surroundings shining through. His mouth turned upward once more, now filled with two opposing rows of teeth, each tooth as sharp as a dagger and twice as pointed. His eyes remained the same, one glowing orange, the other hidden under an eye patch designed to look like a button. A half dozen additional Insolence Eyes had sprung up across his top hat—whether joining or replacing the singular flower, Ben could not tell.

The figures in front of Ben had begun to change as well, their features twisting and their bodies warping. They began to lurch forward, their glowing red eyes

trained on Ben with dangerous intent. "I have but one thing to leave you with; stay out of my business," the Entity's giant form barked. "If you continue to follow your current path, you will live to regret it."

With that, the Entity was gone without so much as a trace, leaving Ben alone to be mauled by his former friends. The creature that used to be Badgy reached out for Ben, its green, glowing arm grabbing him by the shoulder roughly. Ben screamed, eyes flying open as he was suddenly jolted awake from his dream.

"Whoa!" Badgy cried out, yanking his arm back from its place on Ben's shoulder. He had been trying to jostle the poor kid awake for a while now, and even Billy and Ollie had woken from their exhaustion-fueled bout of shut-eye.

"You okay?" Ben scanned the train for any sign of the Iniquitous One, and then once more for any sign of Officer Doggy or Sally, but he came up empty-handed on both fronts. Ben could not gauge how long he had been asleep, but judging by the way that the lights on the train had turned off, the subway car had long since come to a stop. They were at the Metro station closest to The Safe Place, meaning that Willow would be waiting for them—likely not with an abundance of patience. The leader of The Silver Paw no doubt had an insane and dangerous task for Ben and his friends; maybe it was for the best that

Ben had gotten as much sleep as he could, no matter how restless it might have been.

"I'm fine . . ." Ben muttered finally, trying to convince his friends as well as himself. He brushed off their concerned looks with a wave of his hands. "Just had a bad dream, that's all."

PIGGY:HUNT

"**H**alt!" came a loud cry, ringing out against the late-night sky. The Silver Paw guards turned their flashlights on the quartet of heroes, Ben bringing his hand to the level of his eyes to stop from being blinded by the twin beams of light. The two guards put their weapons away sheepishly as lights illuminated the faces of the heroes who were saving Lucella from the Infection. "Aw jeez, guys," said one of the guards, running back to his station and pulling a zip cord from his waist, entering a purple key into a lock. "We didn't know it was you."

"Can't be too careful," asserted the other, ambling back to her own station and pulling an identical but orange key from a zip cord at her belt. "Not with all those nutjobs running around out there." The two guards turned their keys simultaneously, the massive steel gate between The Safe Place and the lawlessness outside it creaking open to admit them. The guards continued to apologize profusely, even as they closed the gate behind the quartet and resumed their posts.

Ben let out a sigh as the gate closed behind them, a deep exhalation of breath he didn't even know that he had been holding in. The Safe Place was just that: the safest place in all Lucella. That was in no small part thanks to the efforts of The Silver Paw, who acted as security for The Safe Place. In the interest of keeping The Safe Place safe, a pair of guards had been stationed at every entrance, with another set of guards situated on the roof. Since the development of the cure, The Silver Paw guards had all taken to carrying

dart guns loaded with the cure, their specialized training making the guards all too effective at neutralizing anything that threatened the welfare and well-being of the safe haven that the survivors had established.

Ben pulled his keycard out of the front pocket of Officer Doggy's backpack, the keypad chirping affirmatively as he entered the code correctly. It was just another in The Safe Place's endless lines of defense against the Infected. Ben warmed almost instantly as he stepped inside, the door shutting slowly behind them and locking out the crisp Lucella evening air. Ben knew that it was only a matter of time before word made its way to Willow that the quartet were back from their latest foray.

The group members broke off from one another, each with a different set of priorities. Chief among those for Ben included bathing his last adventure off him and stuffing his face. The food at The Safe Place was not likely to win any prestigious awards anytime soon, but it was practically five-star quality compared to the water bottles and cans of beans scattered around the intercity. After his dinner—or maybe it was lunch this time, it all began to blur together after a while—he made a few rounds throughout The Safe Place, making sure to stop by and see his parents as well as Badgy's little siblings, just in case you were wondering what happened to them.

Ben's "free time" was short-lived. A summons for him blared over the building-wide intercom system, not-so-gently requesting his presence in the third-floor conference room.

It was less a conference room than an old storage space that Willow had cleared out and filled with maps of Lucella and old whiteboards, but Ben had to admire Willow's tenacity. The others were already there when Ben arrived. Ollie sat slumped in a chair in the corner, Billy leaned against the wall—not brave enough to test if the chairs here would support his massive frame, and Badgy paced back and forth so impatiently, he threatened to wear his path into the floor.

"Well, well, well . . . Look at these familiar faces!" Willow remarked as Ben entered the room, dozens of Silver Paw agents having already arrived, milling about as they drained a steel drum full of coffee. "So glad you could join us." Willow stood behind a wooden podium at the head of a long steel slab of a table, a weary but determined look gracing her lupine features.

Ben supposed that if he had been tasked with leading an island-wide resistance against the scourge of monsters attacking Lucella, then the stress may have begun to show on his face as well. The fur on Willow's face was grayer than Ben remembered it, though her cheeks were just as maroon. She wore her usual all-black outfit—dark pants and a black combat scarf and jacket wrapped over a purple shirt. Willow had once accidentally let slip that the scarf she wore had once belonged to her younger brother, a wolf named William, but she had not been too forthcoming about her sibling's fate. Ben could guess why. If there was more to know about Willow, she kept it close.

Ben nodded in acknowledgment to the leader of The Silver Paw and waved slightly, taking a seat in the corner of the room next to Ollie. Willow took a long swill from her own cup of coffee, draining it in one fell swoop and setting her paper cup down on the edge of her podium. She cleared her throat, the lights in the room dimming as one of the Silver Paw agents fired up a projector, the machine coughing to life with a dull whirring sound. A square of white light illuminated the far wall next to Willow, a fuzzy image slowly sharpening until a map of Lucella was projected onto the wall. Willow gestured around the map as she spoke, using what appeared to be a collapsible metal car antenna as a pointer.

"This, as you all know, is the island of Lucella," Willow began, circling the island with her pointer as she walked back and forth in front of the projector. "And this . . ." Willow crossed to the right side of the screen, her pointer thwacking loudly on the wall as she directed everyone's attention to a small green dot on the map. "This is The Safe Place." Ben had already begun to zone out, losing his grip on concentration as his eyes scanned the map for familiar sites and landmarks.

Ben had started his journey on the northwest side of the island. That was where the map placed the suburb

that Ben and Ollie lived in, as well as the police station where he had met Officer Doggy, and the school where he had rescued Sally. Officer Doggy and Ben had driven to the city, the car running out of gas just outside the Lucella Art Gallery. A small patch of trees on the map denoted the forest on the southwestern outskirts of town, where Ben had spent several nights after losing Officer Doggy. It struck Ben just how close everything looked on this map, as if you could saunter from one place to another. Before The Silver Paw had cleared out the Metro system, even the simplest of expeditions could take days on foot, longer if the way was blocked by swarms of the Infected. Sometimes it was easier to take the long way around than risk waking a nest of the infected creatures. Willow continued to go over the map, pointing out clusters of the Infected and advising the agents of The Silver Paw present at the meeting.

"And here . . ." Willow struck the map with her pointer, a loud metallic and reverberating **THWAP!** sound piercing the air and bringing Ben's attention back to the commander. "Here is where we've traced the signal back to."

Ben's eyes refocused on the map, finding where Willow's metal pointer had landed. The point was circling a small area on the northeastern side of the island. It was a part of Lucella that he was not as familiar with, but to be fair, no one was. There was nothing out there but an old abandoned lab and military outpost, both of which had fallen into disuse after the advent of the Infection. Every couple of months, a traveling carnival would come through Lucella and set up shop there, but even then, you could travel to that by taking the railway. There was nothing out there but wilderness. Wilderness and the Infected.

As if reading his mind, Willow moved her pointer, gesturing toward a cluster of red dots encircling and enshrouding that section of the map. Those, she explained to the gathered Silver Paw agents, were infection hot spots—places where her intelligence had noted a large or overwhelming presence of infected creatures.

"But we think there's a reason for that," Willow stated, clearing her throat once again as the projector clicked to the next slide. The map of Lucella shrank and expanded, the next slide focusing on only the small portion of the map containing the danger zone of Lucella. From this perspective, the cluster of Infected were even greater. Willow collapsed her pointer in her hand, draining her second cup of hot coffee. "We think this is where it all began."

Ben sat up in his seat, finally paying Willow his full attention. Now he knew why she had found this meeting to be so urgent, why she had called him and his friends back from their work in the field. If they had really found out where this infection had started, maybe they could finally put an end to this whole thing and go back to their normal lives. If there were such a thing anymore.

"So, what's the idea?" Ben blurted out, forgoing proper etiquette by not raising his hand. "We fight our way through a swarm of monsters, find out what's making everyone sick, and save the day?"

"Hm, an excellent plan, Ben," Willow commended the young man, clicking through to the next slide on her projector. "Thank you for volunteering." Badgy groaned from the opposite side of the room, knowing that anywhere that Willow sent Ben, she was sure to send him as well. Ben brought his face to his palm, almost disappointed he had not seen that result coming.

"Not to worry, Ben," Willow chirped. "We've picked up some radio signals coming from that area. If I'm not mistaken, you may be about to reunite with an old friend." Willow nodded at one of the agents of The Silver Paw, who pressed play on a recording. The message was garbled and tinny, but Ben would know that voice anywhere. He had first heard it months and months ago, yet it still cropped up in his dreams from time to time. Ben stood out of his seat, crossing the room to the device and pressing his ear to it, trying to make out the message as best he could. It did not make much sense, some sort of rambling about testing, but Ben knew that voice.

"Mr. P?" Ben asked, his upward inflection denoting a question he already knew the answer to. Willow nodded solemnly in response. "How do you know—?"

Willow held up a single finger to silence his question, answering only with the same cryptic phrase that she always did. "Eyes and ears, Ben. Eyes and ears." Willow cleared her throat once more, and once more the projector switched slides, the machine humming softly as it worked. An image appeared on the wall, dozens of blurry infected creatures. All shapes and sizes, each of them bearing a red glowing eye. Ben remembered his dream and shivered. A hushed murmur ran through the crowd of gathered Silver Paw agents. Half of them had been here for months, meaning they had not seen an infected creature in person for a good long while, if ever. The other half were trained to fight with the Infected and had seen enough of them to last a lifetime. It was eerie seeing the Infected with the ability to roam freely without being curtailed. It was almost as if the Infected had turned an entire quadrant of the island into their own personal safe place. Any Infected that dared wander to The Safe Place were instantly hit with a cure dart and brought inside to sleep it off. Ben couldn't imagine that an uninfected wandering over the infected creatures' borders would be treated with the same hospitality.

Ben averted his eyes from the blurry, blown-up display. He had seen enough gnashing teeth and swiping claws. It was not something that a person got used to, ever, and now they had a chance to make sure that no one would ever have to. And if what the Entity had told him in his dreams was true . . . No. Ben shook his head, clearing the thought from his mind. It had just been a dream, right? Either way, it was best to leave it at that.

Ollie, however, seemed unphased by the imagery on the screen before him. He snorted derisively, scoffing at the cluster of infected creatures.

"Bring 'em on," he cried out to no one in particular. The eyes of every Silver Paw agent in the room fell on Ollie, but despite his age, he had just as much experience in this fight against the Infected as anyone in this room—maybe more. While Ben had been running around with Officer Doggy and taking rescue missions from strangers, Ollie had been out surviving in the wilderness of Lucella. Ollie— not Ben, Badgy, Billy, or even the tough-as-nails Willow—was the only one here who had succumbed to the Infection and come back from it. If Ollie said that he could handle the swarm, Ben believed him.

"It's like in a ninja movie, right?" Ollie asked the room. "It's only a problem if you're fighting a ninja one-on-one. The more ninjas there are, the more likely you are to wipe the floor with them. Seriously, no one here has seen—?"

"Yeah, but if youse get attacked by a ninja, you don't *turn into* a ninja," Badgy countered, rolling his eyes. Ollie did some quick work in his head. It was true, being a ninja did come with a certain degree of non-transference. "Whatever. We've been up against worse. Did you all forget about—OW!"

Ben kicked Ollie under the table, perhaps a bit harder than he had intended. The last thing that they needed was for Willow to find out and freak out about the concept of an intelligent uncurable giant mutant creature. That seemed like the kind of news that would warrant another late-night meeting or worse—another slideshow. Ollie winced as he massaged his shin.

"You know kids . . ." Ben explained, shrugging off the bewildered looks from Willow and the agents of

The Silver Paw. "I hear they say the darndest things." Ben kicked Ollie again under the table, the younger of the two adventurers giving Willow and the agents a pained thumbs-up.

". . . right," Willow concluded. Her brow furrowed inquisitively, but she thankfully did not press the issue any further. She cleared her throat, the projector clicking off and the lights coming up. "Get some rest, you four," Willow advised to Ben, Badgy, Billy, and Ollie as the Silver Paw agents filed out of the planning room, trudging back to their usual posts. "You leave first thing in the morning."

The next morning, more so than any other, it took Ben a while to force himself out of bed. Maybe Ben was just lazy. Maybe, like most teenagers, he needed a good eight to ten hours of sleep each night to function at his best. Most likely, however, Ben found it difficult to get out of bed because his time at The Safe Place was the only time in which he got to use one. He had grown so used to sleeping with his head on a felled tree trunk or curled up against Badgy's fur or Billy's stomach or, if he was lucky, with Officer Doggy's backpack balled up beneath his head. Ben had almost forgotten how it felt to lay his head down on a real pillow, and these days, a mattress was worth its weight in tokens. Which would actually be quite a lot, given how heavy a good mattress could be. Ben physically pushed himself from his bed, worried that if he lay there for even a moment longer, he would sink into the scratchy woolen sheets and never leave.

He changed into freshly laundered clothes and poured himself a tin of cold beans—the constant meal du jour at The Safe Place and the postapocalyptic breakfast of champions. Washing out his tin of beans with hot running water—yet another luxury provided by The Safe Place—Ben placed it in the proper receptacle to be recycled. Through eyes still heavy lidded and bleary with exhaustion, Ben slowly traipsed back up the stairs to The Safe Place's living quarters. While not palatial by any means, The Safe Place still boasted enough space to shelter both the displaced and the newly uninfected of Lucella, which in times like these was more than enough to be grateful for.

Ben brushed his teeth for the recommended two-and-a-half minutes, then flossed his teeth and rinsed his mouth with water, spitting the excess into the sink and watching it swirl down the drain, then disappear. There was a metaphor there somewhere, but Ben was far too tired to search for it. He cupped the running water in his hands, bringing the cold liquid to his face and splashing himself repeatedly. Drying himself with a towel, he looked at his reflection in an old mirror, marred with dust—likely a holdover from whatever this place had been before The Silver Paw had taken it over and turned it into a sanctuary for the people of Lucella.

The splash of cold water had not had the invigorating effect that Ben had been hoping for. If anything, he felt more worn out than ever before. Maybe this was who Ben was now, maybe "tired" was simply part of his personality. Perhaps perpetual exhaustion was unskippable, like a cutscene in an online computer game—an unmissable, inevitable stepping stone in the journey to adulthood. Ben shook his head vigorously in an effort to clear some of his more tiring thoughts from his head. As much as he wished to the contrary, no one had ever come across even a momentary burst of energy by ruminating on how tired they were. Ben finished washing up, grabbed his favorite black leather jacket off a hook, and headed down the stairs to the lobby. Ollie, Billy, and Badgy were already in the lobby waiting when Ben rounded the corner down the stairs. He would not have thought it possible, but the other three looked just as exhausted as he felt. It seemed that the unparalleled bliss provided by a good night's sleep could just as easily be snatched away by the blue funk and anxiety of an early morning. It was far too early in the morning to exchange pleasantries; instead the boys nodded at one another in the affirmative, communicating in the way that men so often did in the mornings—through a series of unintelligible grunts.

Ben tried unsuccessfully to stifle a yawn as the quartet pushed through the heavy steel-colored doors of The Safe Place, making their way outside. A pair of guards, different than the ones from the previous evening, inserted a set of identical color-coordinated keys into a console and turned them simultaneously. The purple and orange keys worked in tandem, activating a mechanism that in turn rolled back the heavy steel gate—the only barrier between The Safe Place and the chaos that currently engulfed the once peaceful and serene island of Lucella. The signature chill in the air caught Ben off guard and he grabbed the excess material of his leather jacket, pulling it tighter around his shoulders. He remembered doing the same thing when he had first stepped out of his house and into this world of nightmare creatures. He had grown into the jacket since then. Sleeves that had once been kept bunched now just barely covered his wrists, and he could feel the thick fabric on his shoulders.

Somewhere in there was another metaphor that Ben was too tired to explore. It was amazing to think that a journey that he had never expected to take him beyond his neighbor's doorstep had now taken them both farther than they ever thought possible.

Ben straightened his back and nodded wordlessly to his companions as The Safe Place's gate closed behind them with a definitive and reverberating **CLANG,** Ollie giving the five-story building that was now home to nearly half of Lucella a wistful glance over his shoulder. He knew, of course, that the quadrumvirate would return, but not until they had

completed their mission and saved the island of Lucella. You know . . . again.

If Willow had sent Ben, Ollie, Badgy, and Billy off from The Safe Place first thing in the morning with the goal of granting them a few extra hours of sunlight, her plan had been a massive failure. The sun had finally risen after the foursome of adventurers had spent a substantial length of time trudging through the cold, wet dew, but it was fighting with the thick blanket of fog carpeting the island—and the sun seemed to know that this was a battle that it could not win. Still, it was a valiant effort on the part of the sun; Ben knew better than anyone the strength it took to keep shining in a world determined to be dark. In regard to a "*plan*" to "*save the world*," Ben would be the first to admit that they did not have one. Not that any of them would have confided this information in Willow or any of the agents of The Silver Paw, but it was quickly becoming clear to Ben that a large part of heroism was ad-libbed.

The young champions of Lucella were making it up as they went along. As Badgy would put it, they were flying by the seats of their pants—widely regarded by many as far and away the best part of the pants to fly by as the seat often contained the pockets. It had long since been the group's modus operandi—their standard operating procedure—to wing it and hope for the best. Somehow, that way of doing things had not yet ended in their untimely and ghastly demise. Badgy and Billy had been working together since before Ben had met them. The two acted as a well-oiled machine—a Rube Goldberg machine—the two triggering each other's actions in impractically overcomplicated and often ridiculous ways. Though it may take a while, and almost certainly not how one would expect, they always met their goal. Badgy was resourceful and a quick thinker. In the situations where that was not enough, Billy, while a bull, was as strong as an ox—the difference really coming down to nomenclature. On the off chance they came across something that Badgy couldn't outthink and Billy couldn't hit with a solid metal piece of weight training equipment, Ollie had picked up an impressive range of survival skills during his time alone in Lucella.

And of course there was Ben. Ben, who was . . . very good at choosing friends. Ben's stomach growled loudly, a pathetic gurgling sound cutting through the midmorning silence. He couldn't know exactly how long it had been since his last meal, but a growing boy could hardly survive off a single tin of beans. Since the only way to get to the northeastern side of the island was by railway, the group agreed to stock up on food first. According to the map Willow had insisted they take with them, there was a grocery store right near the train station. They could stock up on food and other supplies before they made their way to the other side of the island. Saving the island again? That was no problem. Saving the island on an empty stomach? That would be a tougher sell.

Fortunately, this time around, their journey on the underground train was an uneventful one. Ben supposed if any of the Metro stations were going to be clear of the Infected, it would be the one closest to The Safe Place. They once again ducked beneath the Metro station turnstiles as public transit is for the people and therefore should be cost-effective. The twelve minutes advertised by the illuminated sign hanging overhead came and went without incident, giving way to the telltale metallic rattling that announced the arrival of the latest train. The once-polished silver train car rattled into the station weakly but on schedule. The plexiglass doors slid open with an exhausted **WOOSH** and the four boys hurriedly entered the train carriage. Ben took the lead, checking the length of the train car just in case any infected creatures had recently decided on a change in scenery. Satisfied the car was in the clear, the group let out a collective sigh as feet, paws, and hooves found their way up onto the seats. They let out another group sigh, this time a different kind of relief. The automated voice rang out over the train's speakers, crackling as it sounded.

## STAND CLEAR OF THE CLOSING DOORS.

Ben grabbed a pole overhead and stood. It had been a long morning and his legs were already feeling the strain of the journey, but it was a short trip to the grocery store and he would rather stand than risk

falling asleep again. Even now, he couldn't help but look over his shoulder for the distorted monster from the other night, certain that he saw those horrible red glowing eyes in every tunnel that they passed through. The train carriage wobbled to a halt at the next Metro station and the doors shuddered open and closed behind the four young men as they disembarked. A moment later, the train was on its way to the next stop, metallic clattering echoing through the tunnel as it went.

Ben had not been to this particular Metro station in a while, and judging by the appearance of it, neither had anyone else. Every surface of the station was covered in spray paint and graffiti, dozens upon dozens of long stretches of interweaving paint lines overlapping and spreading throughout the station. Ollie stopped by a particularly impressive piece of script, five letters scrawled beneath a picture of someone carrying a baseball bat. Ollie quirked a brow in confusion. "Gurty? What is that even supposed to mean?"

"Probably someone's idea of a joke," Ben replied, heading up the long defunct escalator, more commonly known as stairs. "Let's get moving." Ben didn't like the idea of staying in one place for too long. It made him nervous, and he found himself constantly looking for exits—a process that was surprisingly both quick and easy in an underground subway station, where the exits were clearly labeled. Ben and his friends followed the exit signs through the underground tunnel, marveling at the massive murals scattered throughout.

"Whoa."

Ollie had come to an abrupt halt in front of a massive spread of graffiti in an unfortunately familiar pattern. Someone had taken their time with this one—two colossal eyes of black, spattered paint stared at the group from the wall, one featuring a glaring, blaring, flaring burst of red. A white iris in the center of the red eye underlined the point that was sprayed out in five-foot-tall black graffiti letters at the base of the mural, in case the artist's point had not been made. A warning, an ominous fact of life: HE'S ALWAYS WATCHING!

The word "always" in the center was written in red, punctuated even more so by the sloppy splatters of paint from the artist's previous runs of paint. In case the message had not been properly driven home, spray-painted eyebrows turned downward gave the eyes an angry look of constant vigilance. So it was true, what they were saying back at The Safe Place. The Entity had been persuasive enough to form his

own fanatical following, and worse yet, they had access to spray paint. A chill ran down Ben's spine and he shivered visibly, glancing around the Metro station and wondering if the eyes he saw floating

79

ominously in the distance were real or a figment of his ever-creeping imagination. Either way, Ben had no intention of sticking around to find out. He urged the group to get moving once more and they obliged, making their way up the stalled escalator steps.

Willow's map had been largely accurate, and it did not take the quartet long to reach the grocery store. This supermarket was connected to the station by a large parking lot, obviously mostly defunct by now. The few cars littered around the lot had long since been abandoned, mostly serving as level decoration and potential hiding spots for the infected creatures. Fortunately, they ran into no resistance once they exited the Metro station, causing Ollie to wonder aloud if maybe all the Infected in this area had already been cleared out by agents of The Silver Paw. This was not the case, it seemed; the sound of infected creatures growling started to fill the air as the grocery store's large, partially illuminated sign began to loom in sight. The boys all stiffened, each of them suddenly on high alert. They had been through this same thing more than once at this point; even the sound of the Infected's wails were enough to make their respective hairs and furs stand on end. Ben's stomach growled again, a pained gurgling sound that drowned out the dreadful grunting coming from inside the grocery store. Ollie, Badgy, and Billy all looked at him and he nodded resolutely, securing Officer Doggy's pack to his back and setting off down the hill. Billy hefted his barbell with one hand and Badgy shouldered his crossbow as he joined, the four of them making their way across the parking lot. As it always seemed to go in situations like these, Ben ended up taking point, leading the four young men across the parking lot.

The fog that blanketed the island made it impossible to truly tell what time it was, only that it was dark, as always. Ben had long since learned that the giant tactical flashlight that Officer Doggy had left to him worked better as a melee deterrent than an actual source of light. In that capacity, it seemed to only attract attention, which was the last thing that Ben and his crew wanted. They reached the clear sliding doors of the grocery store, and Ollie cupped his hands around his eyes and peered through the doors to see inside. Predictably, the place was full of the creatures, some rummaging among the heavily ransacked shelves, some stuffing their grotesque faces with food long past its expiration date, and dozens of others just sleeping. The growling that they had heard across the parking lot was, in fact, the sound of snoring. Ben quickly lost count of just how many creatures were spread throughout the grocery store, but he would not be deterred from his goal. Mainly because he wasn't sure his stomach would hold out until the four of them could make their way to the next grocery store on the map. Taking a deep breath and steeling himself for whatever was to come next, he stood in front of the automatic doors. To Ben's surprise, they did not slide open for him. The doors seemed to not even recognize his presence. He looked around to his team, shrugging as he waved his hand in front of the sensor once again, to no avail.

## KERR-ASH!

The sound of thousands of shards of broken glass

hitting one another and then the ground rang out, piercing through the chorus of snores from the infected creatures. The final pieces of the glass door hit the ground, ringing out with the soft tinkle of a wind chime being softly blown on a cool spring day. Then came the silence. You could hear a pin drop, though after a bull throwing a weighted barbell through the window, dropping a pin as well may be a bit superfluous. Billy reached through the door and grabbed his barbell, brushing off small pieces of glass before maneuvering his hand to unlock the grocery store from the inside. The latch clicked and the lock opened, what remained of the door swinging open to grant them admittance.

"Honestly, what kind of a person would lock the door to a grocery store behind them?" Billy asked, breaking the eerie silence. The silence was better than the snoring, but at least the snoring had let the quartet know that they were safe. The infected creatures began to stir, the sound of metal being thrown through glass an effective alarm for even the most tired and lethargic of mindless monsters. Two floating red eyes flickered into four, then eight, each dry blink of a creature's eyes seeming to spawn an identical one somewhere in the background. The doors to the grocery store had not been barred shut to keep fellow survivors out, but to keep in this particular cluster of the Infected. Work that had all been deftly undone by Billy in a single, shattering blow.

Badgy raised his crossbow to the level of his eyes, aiming down the scope before firing off three rounds of cure darts. They struck true, needle tips finding purchase in the rough skin of the Infected as they dropped back to the ground, snoring hard, the cure pumping through their veins and purging them of the Infection. But even Badgy, as prolific a shot as he was, could not put down all the creatures. A wave of the Infected began to bear down on them, clambering over the sleeping bodies of the cured. The chase, it seemed, was already underway. Dozens of pale, stubby arms reached through the shattered door, each wandering hand seeking uninfected flesh to bite. Ben pulled Officer Doggy's taser from his pack, but anyone with a hint of common sense could tell that they would be overwhelmed sooner rather than later, even if Ben did manage to shock one or two of the monsters into submission. It was a losing battle already and they had not even begun.

"Run!" Ben cried out before turning tail to the tainted creatures and picking up his legs as he broke into a brisk run. His friends followed suit quickly behind, each of them increasing their pace to a run as they felt the hot breath of the infected creatures bearing down on them. The way ahead was blocked—shattered glass and a half dozen or so creatures sleeping off their infection lay across the entrance of the grocery store—and a growling swarm of the Infected stood between our heroes and the supermarket. Ben turned, leading his friends and thus the army of Infected toward the back of the grocery. Ben pushed up against the first door that he came across, bouncing off the wooden frame with just as much force as he had exerted. Locked, of course. That was just Ben's rotten luck. Billy, on the other hand, had never experienced an obstacle he could not plow through in one way or another, and this would turn out to be no exception.

Already in a galloping run, Billy gathered speed and rammed the door with the full weight of his body, the door collapsing inward with a heavy, resounding slam. Billy was gifted in a great many ways; stealth was not one of them. The quartet of heroes filed in one after another—Billy, Ben, Ollie, and Badgy bringing up the rear, covering their rears with whatever cure vials he could manage to load into his crossbow. Several of the infected creatures fell to his efforts but it was no use, each vial of the cure administered having all the effect of attempting to quell the sun with a water pistol. They didn't bother trying to barricade the door, instead moving through the back room of the grocery, dozens of the infected creatures still bearing down on them.

Ben dared not look back and count, but if the echoing growls and thudding footsteps were any indication, they were being pursued by many more of the Infected than Ben would have liked. Ollie pushed over a stack of boxes in an attempt to impede the creatures' advancing progress. Another futile gesture as the infected creatures were not exactly agile, instead

seemingly much more interested in lumbering through any obstacles in their paths.

Billy burst through another door, the foursome finding themselves in the grocery store. Taking quick stock of his surroundings, Ben felt his stomach drop.

The only exits were on opposite sides of the building, and the aisles sprawled out in a labyrinthine manner, making Ben wonder whether the store's designer had intended for this to be difficult. They split up as they entered the store, the level design allowing them more space to maneuver and, more importantly, to outmaneuver. The infected creatures poured in two to three at a time, often getting stuck in the doorframe as their all-encompassing and insatiable hunger won out over simple concepts like single-file lines. In the excitement of it all, Ben lost track of his companions. When the four of them split up, so, too, did the infected creatures, each of the mindless monsters dragging their decrepit bodies toward the person closest to them. A few aisles down, Ben heard the familiar clang of Billy's steel barbell; he felt confident that the bull could take care of himself.

Ben shuffled around in Officer Doggy's backpack as he continued to move away from the creatures; his only option at this point was to be where they were not. Fingers closing around a cool plastic handle, he pulled Officer Doggy's old taser from the bag. It wasn't as sturdy as stainless-steel weightlifting equipment and not as flashy as a crossbow, but it had gotten him out of a few scrapes before, and its work wasn't yet done. The device powered up with a high-pitched whir, a small green light letting Ben know that it had reached its full charge. Ben aimed the device at the creature nearest to him and tensed his finger on the mechanism, an electrified barb ejecting from its cartridge and striking true, shocking the thing into submission. A rational creature would have ended the pursuit there, having seen the results of the first creature's attempt to make a meal out of Ben. The Infected were not rational creatures.

They stepped over their stunned friend, though the creature would only be out of commission for ten seconds, perhaps twenty if Ben was lucky. It was a fact that did not work in the young man's favor. He continued moving through the aisles, confronted each time he rounded a corner by the hot, heaving breath of another of the abominable creatures. One of the Infected swiped at Ben. He ducked at the last second, the creature colliding with another of the Infected as Ben slipped between them without incident, but Ben was running out of room to outmaneuver the creatures and he could only loop around so many times before they boxed him in. A looming presence over his shoulder caused him to whip around sharply, Officer Doggy's taser whining loudly as Ben primed the small, handheld device to fire once more. He looked up, surprised to see a pair of heterochromatic eyes—one blue, one green looking back down at him, instead of the haunting red eyes that had menaced his every waking moment since this whole thing had begun.

"Billy!" Ben exclaimed, throwing his arms around as much of his enormous friend as he could fit his arm span around. Hugging his friend, he could see how the bull had fared against the infected creatures. At least a half dozen of the monstrous animals were unconscious and strewn about the aisle behind Billy, each of them bearing the telltale bruises of having lost a battle with a barbell.

"We have to find Ollie," Ben said single-mindedly, releasing Billy from the tight grip of his embrace. Billy raised a hooved hand, gesturing somewhere in the distance behind Ben.

"I don't know. It looks like he's doing all right for himself."

Ben's eyeline followed to where Billy was pointing, and sure enough, Ollie was doing just fine. Pressing his back against the glass doors of the frozen food section, Ollie barred the doors with what looked to be a discarded mop handle. The infected creatures on the other side of the doors struggled against the barricade, but it was a useless endeavor against the broom handle and Ollie's leverage against the freezer doors. It took several moments, but the creatures began to fall one by one as they succumbed to exhaustion and the cold, a splashy wooden sign hanging above the freezer section advertising FROZEN PORK! becoming more accurate by the second.

Ben had long since abandoned his sense of time, but even still, it felt as if it took forever for the last of them to fall. Eyes still glaring as they fluttered closed, bared teeth chattering, the large animal finally fell to the ground, the heaving breaths of the unconscious Infected turned into a steam that quickly filled the blockaded freezer. Ollie let out his own sigh of relief—the exhalation of yet another breath that he did not realize that he had been holding—as he sank to the ground, exhausted from his considerable efforts. Ben and Billy jogged over to him, Billy admittedly doing most of the work in lifting Ollie back to his feet. The bull gave his friend a pat on the back with his free hand while Ollie caught his breath and wiped sweat from his brow as he dusted off his clothes.

Almost as if in answer to the question that Ben was getting ready to ask, Badgy rounded the corner. His fur was ruffled and his shirt was missing a few of its topmost buttons and the crimson tie that he always wore around his neck was twisted the wrong way, bright red fabric flapping over the badger's left shoulder. Still, Ben had seen Badgy looking more disheveled than this before his morning coffee at The Safe Place, and as Badgy cautiously rolled down his sleeve and buttoned it shut, he seemed no worse for wear.

"Everyone all right?" the badger asked, making sure that everyone was accounted for. The group nodded collectively, checking themselves and one another for any signs of bites or scratches. Satisfied with the results, they finally took stock of the grocery store. Most of the shelves had been stripped bare of their stock. Ollie dragged a finger across the shelves, their true color barely managing to shine through the layers of dirt and grime. If the buildup of dust was any indication, this grocery store hadn't seen business in months, if not longer. There were food wrappers and packaging strewn across the aisles without care, most likely the result of weeks upon weeks of infected creatures setting up shop, for lack of a better word. The Infected were not a particularly discerning bunch and would eat most anything they came across, gorging themselves until they fell asleep, and then waking up and doing the same thing the next day.

The group of four adventurers split up once again, moving from aisle to aisle in their search for food, but finding the same thing in each aisle. Anything useful had long since been torn into, eaten, or otherwise made useless, and anything that was still on the shelves had gone bad so long ago that it may have been more beneficial to their health to simply succumb to the virus. Ben led the group around the grocery store twice, just to make sure they hadn't missed anything. Two tins of tuna, a loaf of bread on its way out, and a questionable can of soup weren't exactly what Ben would label as a victory—and even if they were, split between four people their spoils would last them approximately one afternoon. Ben sat down on the checkout counter and sighed, his face sinking into his hands. His stomach growled, an inopportune moment that seemed to exist only to remind of his failure.

Rubbing his forehead in a mixture of exhaustion, disappointment, and exasperation, Ben suddenly caught a small, metallic glint from the corner of his eye. Ben instantly perked up, his sense of curiosity overwhelming his sense of disappointment if only for a moment. Tucked into the corner, and stacked higher than Ben was tall, was a display of silver cans. The harsh overhead fluorescent lights kept them mostly hidden in the shadows, but every now and then, the fluorescent flickering would sharply throw the cans into the light. Ben pushed himself off the countertop gingerly, hoping against hope that whatever was in the cans was at the very least somewhat edible. He approached the display and grabbed one of the cans; the weight he felt when he picked it up let him know immediately that the can was full. Ben picked up another can, finding it to be full as well. Another can. Then another. And another. And one more just for sport. Each can was as full as the day it had been delivered. Ben almost let a smile grace his boyish face before he saw the label, a familiar image grabbing his attention as he read the small paper wrapped around the can.

These were the same exact beans that he had been eating at The Safe Place. In fact, Ben would not

batch. He put the palm of his hand to his face, unable to keep from sighing loudly into his hand.

"What have you got over there?" Ollie cried out across the grocery store. Ben held up a can in each hand, making sure that the labels were facing outward so that his fellow adventurers would not be disappointed the way that he was. Their faces fell in a similar manner as Ben's, but food was food, and the quartet seemed to be in a considerably better mood as they loaded up Officer Doggy's old pack with as many cans of food as they could comfortably carry. Though it seemed that our heroes were not the only ones in need of sustenance.

A soft, nearly imperceptible tinkling sound came from the front of the grocery store, causing Ben to pause, pulling his arm back out from loading the cans of beans into Officer Doggy's pack. Ben knew that it could have been nothing. In fact, he was relatively sure that most people would not have even noticed the sound. Ben was not most people, not anymore, and any sound he could not instantly identify and locate was likely to set him on edge. Ben's eyes darted to the source of the sound with the trained edge of someone who had been surviving in Lucella for some time. It didn't take long for the source of the noise to identify itself. For the first time since the quartet had left The Safe Place, they were faced with a new horror.

A figure shifted in the darkness, a pair of eyes glinting in the dim overhead fluorescent light. Ben raised a hand to his friends, halting their movement. These eyes weren't the menacing, floating red orbs that Ben had grown accustomed to seeing floating in the night, the kind that rested just behind the heavy lids of the creatures sleeping on the ground all around them. These eyes were orange and alert, and they darted back and forth between Ben, Badgy, Ollie, and Billy nervously, like a child who had been caught with their hand in the cookie jar. This was no child, however. Beneath the nervous orange eyes of the intruder sat an angular face covered in scaly, parsley-colored skin. A light green jaw gave way to a long U-shaped snout ending in two small, slotted nostrils and a mouth full of several dozen three-inch-long, overlapping off-white teeth. Only the top teeth were visible; their

new reptilian friend's upper jaw was wider than their lower jaw, making their bottom teeth disappear when their mouth was closed. Still, the sight of all those teeth was not one that Ben was soon to forget, and the intruder didn't look altogether friendly to begin with.

The reptilian raider adjusted the ill-fitting brown fedora that he wore on the top of his head, fixing the small colored band that ran around the hat as he pulled his dark-brown jacket up around his shoulders. A flat, muscular tail dragged on the ground behind the visitor, and he wore a light-brown shirt over the bony, armored plates embedded in the skin on his back. Slung over the reptile's right shoulder was a dirtied brown messenger bag, tied upright and filled nearly to the point of bursting. The length of rusty pipe that the alligator carried in his right hand led Ben to believe that this was not his first time venturing out into the woods of Lucella.

Ben silently chided himself for allowing them to be sneaked up on. This was the kind of lax leadership that could be brought on by the lack of a proper balanced diet and recommended hours of sleep for a growing boy. Billy had shattered the glass door entrance of the grocery store into a thousand pieces with his steel barbell when they had arrived. At the time, faced with the prospect of a horde of monsters, they had reasonably assumed that their biggest obstacles lay ahead of them. Now these same glass pieces crunched under the foot of their strange visitor. The quartet had all been so busy—a leisurely afternoon of grocery shopping was one thing, grabbing anything that looked edible off the shelves while a violent throng of infected animals tried to induct you into their evil horde was something else entirely—that they had forgotten to barricade the entrance behind them. It was a rookie mistake, and if Officer Doggy's walkie-talkie weren't stuffed in the rucksack on Ben's back, Ben was certain that Willow would be berating him for it on every available wavelength.

The four adventurers' eyes flitted around the room, each of them alternating keeping their eyes glued on the newest addition to their situation and looking to one another to see who among them would be the first to spring into action. It was quickly becoming pain-fully clear that it would be none of them—all four were dumbfounded and rooted to the spot in shock. Infected rage monsters with enhanced strength and insatiable appetites were par for the course these days, but a living, breathing person? It wasn't as if Badgy could just shoot a crossbolt loaded with the cure at their new friend and let him sleep it off. They certainly couldn't begrudge him for stealing from a ramshackle, broken-down old grocery store; were they not here to do the exact same thing themselves? Ben's fingers twitched toward Officer Doggy's pack in practiced anticipation. As long as the alligator didn't move, it seemed the five of them were at an impasse, a veritable Lucellan standoff. It would take Ben only a moment to rifle through his inventory and find the old plastic taser that had already saved his skin countless times before, but Ben made it a point never to incapacitate someone through modulated electrical current if he could offer his hand in peace first. The Safe Place was still just that, a safe place, and anyone who had survived this long on their own in the woods of Lucella was more than welcome to use it as sanctuary. Ben would not get a chance to make his offer.

The alligator made the first move. He had been so perfectly motionless for so long, the sudden movement caught the group by surprise. The reptilian bandit raised and extended his right arm, casting forth his weapon and flinging it at the four heroes assembled before him. The rusty piece of pipe that he had heretofore been gripping tightly to his side went sailing through the air, letting out an undulating whistle as it flew toward them, end over end. Ben's eyes grew wide as the hollow, tubular metal section hurtled past his face, the air displaced by the object grazing his face as it missed narrowly, continuing on to strike Billy in the chest. The pipe bounced off the massive bull, clattering to the ground in front of them with a dull, echoing **CLANG!**

It was the intruder's turn to glance blankly among the four young heroes, his attempt at getting them off his proverbial and literal tail now rolling to a halt in between them. Ben could almost read the stranger's thought process behind his orange eyes, his scaly brows furrowed in concentration.

Ben would never know what the alligator was truly thinking, though, because in that moment, he turned and ran, hurtling over the shattered glass. Ben was more than happy to let the alligator bandit go—he seemed to be more trouble than he was worth, and if there was one thing that Ben was trying to avoid these days, it was trouble. Though despite his best efforts, for the last several months, trouble had seemed to find him. The stranger huffed and puffed as he ran away, his backpack making a distinctive jostling sound as he made his attempt to flee, the clinking of glass and metal and plastic all brushing up against one another. The reason quickly became clear as a jar of food popped out of the intruder's sack and rolled down the hill toward Ben and Ollie. Ollie reached down, picking up the jar and examining the label, as he simultaneously made the same revelation as Ben did but out loud.

"Hey, look!" Ollie shouted, pointing after the man. "That guy's got all the food!" Ben's eyes followed his friend's gesture, finally fully taking in the dirtied brown bag slung over the creature's shoulders. Ollie was correct; the man's backpack was stuffed to the brim with what seemed to be the entire remaining contents of the grocery store's inventory. As if in yearning, Ben's stomach gurgled loudly. His hunger meter was running low, and though he had filled Officer Doggy's pack with cans of food, it would be a dream to fill his stomach up on something other than the same can of beans he could buy at any survivor's camp for five coins. Ben placed a hand over his stomach to quell the agitation, the sound of his hunger subsiding just in time to give way to a chorus of low groans. Of course.

The quartet had been so focused on the scaly bandit that they had forgotten to attend to the infected creatures throughout the grocery store. There was no real way to put out one of the Infected without administering the cure to them, so most methods of incapacitating the creatures involved knocking them unconscious for brief periods of time with something heavy or a sudden fall. Ben reckoned that for the most part, the creatures were only out of it for ten seconds at a time, maybe twenty if they were lucky, but sometimes that was all that you needed. This did not look like it was shaping up to be one of those times.

The groans began to grow louder as more of the creatures started to wake, some of them pushing themselves upright and beginning to lumber toward the quartet. With the food they had come here to retrieve now fading into the distance on an alligator's back, perhaps it was best for them to cut their losses. As more and more of the infected creatures began to rouse from their slumber and lurch toward the heroes, it was looking like now, more than ever, was a good time to make their exit. Ben picked up his feet, shuffling quickly to the entrance and ducking through the busted door, careful to avoid the kaleidoscope of broken glass. Badgy followed suit, moving lithely as always, barely disturbing the glass at all as he slunk his way through the door. As usual, stealth was the least of Billy's concerns.

The bull displayed an almost shocking lack of finesse as he barreled headfirst through the double doors, knocking them asunder. Finally, only Ollie was left among the slowly awakening monsters. The band of the infected creatures that Ollie had managed to trap in the freezer section earlier were beginning to wake, glowing red eyes and cloven, grasping hands pressed against the frost-covered glass. The chorus of ghoulish noises only grew louder as Ollie scuttled across the grocery store's cool tile floor, grabbing the reptilian food thief's old, rusted copper pipe as he moved. Ollie placed one foot in front of the other as quickly as he could, the sound of his footsteps thudding on the floor being nearly drowned out by the cacophonous groans of the Infected and the rattling din of the creatures struggling against barricades. Each frantic breath that he managed to take burned like fire; the young hero's lungs worked overtime, struggling to keep up with Ollie's actions. He was nearly home free, the entrance to the grocery store now looming ever nearer.

From the corners of his eyes, Ollie could see the infected creatures beginning to bear down on him, growing closer and closer with each bedraggled step they took. Ollie had come too far and seen too much to falter now. He himself had been the test subject for the first batch of the cure, having succumbed to the Infection beneath the temple in Doveport at the hands of the gigantic arachnid creature they called Spidella. He still remembered everything—their days had been so packed with action of late, it was easy to forget that it had not been all that long ago. Ollie remembered the shivers that had come over his body, the icy chill that ran through his veins as the virus began to take hold of him. He remembered how heavy the lids of his eyes had felt as he struggled to stay awake, drifting into the dark abyss of unconsciousness. Ollie remembered hearing the voices of his friends—muffled, confused, panicked. And then . . . *nothing*. It was as if during that time, Ollie hadn't experienced a single thing.

He had been floating in the midst of oblivion, somehow less than alive but more than unconscious—truly a nothing person in a nowhere place. That is, until a sharp jab had pierced through the fog and a warm sensation spread through his body, tugging him back to the land of the living. Ollie remembered it all, and it was not at all something that he was eager to experience again.

Ollie was shaken from his detached reverie by a sharp growl, a rumbling roar that came far too close to Ollie's ear for his comfort. One of the creatures drew near to Ollie, exposing its horrible, yellowing teeth. Glowing red eyes throughout the grocery store turned to fixate on Ollie. The monstrous creatures had decimated the grocery's food supply long ago, it was no mystery to Ollie that they saw him as nothing more than sustenance that had unwittingly wandered into their midst. But that would not be Ollie's fate. Not today.

## BONK!

The sound of aging metal against ghoulish, leathered

skin rang out throughout the store as Ollie bashed one of the creatures with the alligator's rusted pipe. Ollie could practically see the flock of cartoon birds circling the creature's head as it pulled back, stunned into stillness with the blow. If the other creatures were at all put off by the predicament of their compeer, they certainly did not let it show, each of the remaining creatures continuing their lurching advancements toward the youngest member of the heroic party.

Ollie reared back once more, ready and more than willing to take on all these creatures all by himself—a young man and a discarded piece of piping alone against a deadly horde. Still, surely there was a better way, and with the swarm of infected creatures bearing down on him and his friends slowly disappearing over the hills in the midst of their frantic chase, a golden opportunity presented itself to Ollie. Ollie ducked, dipped, dove, and dodged away from the dirtied digits of the deranged denizens. The young man was an artist with his movements, an interpretive dance where the only goal was his survival. It seemed so long ago and yet just like yesterday that he

had been alone in the wilds of Lucella, waking up each day to fend for himself in a world where monsters had appeared seemingly overnight.

The creatures here were slow, almost lethargic in comparison, no doubt the result of having all their meals for the last several months plopped directly in front of them. But when dealing with the Infected, even the fastest of them seemed to prioritize sheer brute force and overwhelming numbers over agility. It often felt as if the infected creatures were hoping that their limited brain cells would rub together and create a spark recognizable as anything other than hunger. This was not a problem to which Ollie could relate. His own ingenuity was his constant companion, one that had not let him down yet. The stunned creature fell back into the crowd of advancing Infected, dizzied by the blow, but Ollie knew that these things never lasted.

Ollie broke into a run, the soles of his shoes slapping loudly against the tile grocery store floor. He would only get one chance at this—there would be no do-overs if he didn't nail it. Another creature reached out from the crowd to try to ensnare Ollie, but the young hero was already gone. Dropping his small frame to the ground, Ollie squeezed through the shattered door-frame at the entrance. Shavings of old rust fell from the pipe as Ollie shoved the alligator's aged piece of metal between the doors' handles, barricading the much larger infected creature inside the store, again.

Wave after wave of the horrid things pressed against the door, their combined weight causing the hinges to groan in protest as they pressed against it. The pipe bowed to their assault, bending but not breaking and finally coming to rest, still angled between the doors' latches. Ollie breathed a heavy sigh of relief, letting go of a breath he had not realized he had been holding and pumping his fist up and down in excitement. He truly did love it when a plan came together.

The youngest member of the foursome did not have much time to celebrate his victory. Looking over his shoulder to the horizon, Ollie saw that Ben, Badgy, and Billy were still in hot pursuit of the alligator bandit, the sound of several cans of beans clinking against one another receding over the hills. It did not take Ollie too long to catch up to the rest of the group, the adrenaline from his run-in with the infected creatures still coursing through his body.

PIGGY:HUNT

Certainly, the fact that Ben had been saddled with a bag full of metal and beans was not helping with his speed. Ben adjusted the bag on his back and wiped sweat from his brow with the back of his hand, eyes dead set and focused on the reptile currently weaving back and forth ahead of them in the distance. Ben would have shouted, but with every step his heart threatened to burst out of his chest. With every breath, his lungs felt like fire. It wasn't really about the food—this alligator was one of maybe half a dozen people that Ben had seen over the last few months who was not actively trying to eat him. If they could catch this guy, maybe have a conversation, they could direct him to The Safe Place, where he would never have to steal food to survive again. Sure, The Safe Place had its rules, its curfews, but it beat trying to survive in the wilds of Lucella by a country mile.

The quartet was gaining ground on the gluttonous gator, each step bringing them closer. The gator was running out of places to run to. There were four people on his tail, and ahead of him only a series of vertical iron bars leading into Lucella's sewer system. The bandit would have had to have been insane to go in there, and yet . . . the alligator froze at the entrance, the metal bars barring his progress. Orange reptilian eyes shifted from side to side as the creature was cornered, the group of heroes finally catching up to him. The gator tried to squeeze between the metal bars leading to the sewer, pushing himself through to no avail. But it seemed the creature had one last trick up its tweed-coated sleeve. He took the sack full of food off his back and shoved it against the bars, using all his weight to force the backpack through.

His considerable efforts were not put to waste, the backpack squeezing through the bars and falling to the other side with a dull and wet **plop.** The foursome was almost on him, and this was almost certainly a dead end. The iron bars that occluded their progress into the sewers were taller than they were wide and seemed to act as a filter between Lucella's sewage and its trash.

"Come on, man!" Badgy shouted between labored breaths. "You got nowhere to go!" The alligator seemed to disagree. Turning his scaly snout to the sky, the reptilian bandit managed to slip through the bars, grabbing the backpack of food and taking off down the sewer corridor. A splash of receding footsteps echoed throughout the sewers as the quartet stared at one another, each trying to take in what they had just seen. Ollie was first to come to his senses, grunting with exertion as he managed to just barely squeeze himself through the bars. The smell was less than pleasant; sewage, trash, and refuse from all over the city made its way through the Lucella Sewer System and seemingly all ended up here. Ben and Badgy tried to force themselves through, but it was of no use. Billy decided to spare them all the time and abstain.

"There has to be a way in . . ." Ben thought aloud, tapping his hand to his chin. He consulted the map that they had been given by Willow back at The Safe Place. The Lucella Sewer System winded and coiled throughout the island, in a way that was not too dissimilar from the way that the city's Metro operated. If they could cut through the sewer system, they might be able to shave some time off their journey to find the cause of all this.

"All right, Billy," Ben called out, gesturing to the sewer system gates with his hands. "Why don't you go ahead and get us in there." Billy stepped up, his ever-present barbell in hand, stretching his upper body. Since Ben had known Billy, he had never once known the bull's strength to fail, and he was certain that this would be no exception.

"I just want you to know, if we weren't facing some apocalyptic circumstances together, I would never do something like this," Billy grumbled.

"Of course not," Ben replied.

"That thing about the china shop is actually based on a very hurtful stereotype, my mother actually owns several very tasteful piec—"

"You're burnin' daylight!" Badgy interrupted loudly. There were more tactful ways to get his point across, but Badgy was right. What was the point of taking a shortcut if not to save yourself time? There were certainly more accurate ways Badgy could have expressed his impatience—day and night had so long since blurred into a singular and omnipresent gray that Ben rarely had any idea what time it was. He looked to the horizon, but instead of sunlight peering over the clouds or moonlight glancing off the vista, he was greeted only by the sight of a hideous red eye in the distance.

It was the distorted, decaying creature from the Metro station—Ben was absolutely sure of it. From a distance, all the Infected looked largely the same, but Ben recognized this one, and that fact did little to give him comfort. A chill ran down his spine as he turned away from those horrible eyes floating on the hillside. When he turned back, predictably, the eyes were gone. Ben wasn't sure if he felt comfort in no longer being able to see the eyes in the distance, or unsettled because he never knew where they disappeared to. Still, just because he could not see the eyes did not mean that they were not still watching him. Ben clapped his hands together, refocusing everyone's attention on him.

"Badgy's right, big guy. Time to step up." Billy nodded solemnly at Badgy and Ben, quite literally stepping up to the bars. Removing the metal plates from his steel barbell, with Ollie's help from the other side, he slid them through the bars. Now wielding a large metal pole, the large bull slid that through the bars, then turned it horizontally. Billy began to pull, the bars groaning in protest against Billy's assault. The iron bars soon gave way—steel, concrete, and dust raining down as the gateway fell through. Trash

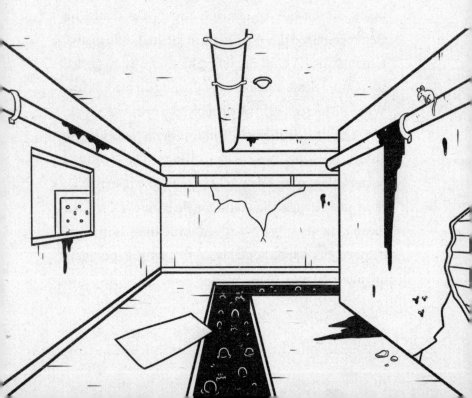

tumbled from the lip of the sewer gate down to their feet, Badgy making a face as he realized just what he was about to have to wade through. Ben couldn't blame him; the smell of the sewer rolled out to greet them as it intermingled with the cool night or possibly early morning air. Ben took one more deep breath of crisp, unadulterated air before adjusting the bag on his back and heading into the sewers.

The Lucella Sewer System was a sprawling map of interweaving and overlapping tunnels and piping, all designed to keep the waste of Lucella moving. Spray-painted graffiti covered the walls, some of it matching the art that they had seen in the Metro station tunnels, but as the four young heroes made their way through the giant concrete tunnels, they discovered that more and more of the graffiti seemed to be dedicated to the Iniquitous One. Ben was not necessarily surprised by this revelation; it only made sense that his followers would seek out one another and band together, and though Ben personally would have chosen a more fragrant location, he understood why the sewer system was such an appealing hideout. They were a group of zealots following the ideations of a nightmare man, so it only made sense for them to find a place to plot and plan, a place where no one would follow them or even think to look in the first place. It was a plan that was almost brilliant in its simplicity.

Almost. The quartet held their noses as they walked, every now and then passing a hastily scrawled note, or an Eye of Insolence spray-painted on the wall. Loud whispers seemed to come from all over, echoing against the cavernous concrete. The source of these whispers was a mystery; any time the boys rounded a corner expecting to come upon a hidden group of the Insolence, they instead found a dead end. Ben was not sure if it was the fumes from the sewage beginning to seep into his brain, but he was almost certain that he could hear his name among the whispers.

The quartet trudged through the sewers for what seemed like hours. The alligator bandit was long gone—if he had ever been through these tunnels to begin with. They passed another piece of graffiti, this time a yellow-and-orange splash project that read only SUBSTANCE-128. Behind the simple symbols was

a drawing of a green liquid, splashing over the lip of a vial. Ben had never heard of Substance-128 or anything like it before, but it sounded ominous and stuck out to him among the rest of the graffiti. While the others seemed like the artistic endeavors of the unwell, this one seemed purposeful. A hint or a warning? Ben swallowed dryly, only shaken from his woolgathering musings by Ollie, who shook his shoulder as the quartet moved on.

Once again, Officer Doggy had proved his worth long after his disappearance, the flashlight that he had left in his backpack now lighting the way for the quartet as they explored the underground sewer system. By Ben's estimation they had already passed a ladder room, a walk-in room, two different engine rooms, and—strangely enough—what appeared to be a classroom. This place was built like a labyrinth and it stunk to the high heavens, but Ben reminded himself that it was still better than facing off with the infected creatures above ground.

They must have gone around in circles at least a dozen times before Ollie noticed it, a small glint of metal catching the light from the corner of his eye. Using Billy as a hoist, Ollie scrambled toward the ceiling, pulling a small white key from between the grates of an air vent. Through the process of elimination, the foursome narrowed down door after door until only one remained. The second engine room's door yielded to the white key, swinging open with an incredibly satisfying click. Still, if they had hoped to find their reptilian friend or a secret cache of useful items, they would be sorely disappointed. There seemed to be nothing in this room but a control panel and a few locked chests—no doubt the keys to open them were stashed around the sewer system.

Ben was in no way surprised to find another dead end; their collective journey had been filled with them. He was about to raise his voice to warn his friends not to touch the control panel, but it was too late. Machinery whirred to life as Ben whipped around to see who had caused the disturbance. Both Badgy and Ollie pointed to Billy, who was sheepishly backing away from the large green button at the center of the console. Through the viewing window of the engine room, Ben watched as an aperture swung open, sewage and trash pouring through it as what seemed like the entire Lucella Sewer System drained through it. The sound was outdone only by the smell, a loud **SCHLORP** as the accumulated waste was dumped out of the gate.

Ben could not believe his eyes. As trash was emptied into the processor, the level of filth in the sewage system began to recede, revealing at first a staircase and then an entire lower level to the sewage complex. What had to have been several tons of muck was flushed from the sewer system, most likely a backup resulting from a lack of upkeep to the facility. That must have been the reason they had seemingly been going in circles all evening; the exit to the facility was on a different level than the entrance, and that level had been obstructed by several months' worth of gunk. Ben congratulated Billy on his genius, excitedly patting the large bull on his back as Ben pushed open the double doors to the engine room. The quartet made their way down the stairs, careful not to slip on the thick layer of sludge that coated every surface. More graffiti marked the walls—more tributes to the Entity and nonsensical conspiratorial scribbling mostly—and the boys used these to mark their progress, a sort of doodled trail of bread crumbs making sure that the boys did not get turned around.

When they finally came upon the exit, it was Badgy who took the lead, bursting through the double doors with gasping, heaving breaths. Badgy was right. Ben was not sure if he had ever taken a breath of air as sweet as this one. The first unpolluted breath that Ben had taken in hours filled his lungs and he was loath to let it go, even to replace it with another. Ben's eyes welled with the beginnings of tears as he tried to remember the last time he had actually been grateful for the crisp Lucella night air. Ben's companions seemed to be experiencing similar sensations, except for Badgy, who was loudly complaining about how long it was going to take to get the smell of the Lucella Sewers out of his fur. *For once*, thought Ben, *Badgy has a valid reason to complain.* Ben let out a sigh of relief. He would let his team rest a moment—they had earned that.

Ben fell to his rear, his knees buckling in exhaustion as he gave his legs their first rest in days. He dug into his backpack, pulling out one of the cans of beans. As if in anticipation, Ben's stomach growled as he rummaged through Officer Doggy's old backpack. The walkie-talkie, Officer Doggy's taser, and a few dozen cans of beans, but not much else. He slipped the walkie-talkie through a loop on his belt. Now that they were out of the sewer system, they were likely to have a better signal. Willow would be wanting a report on the group's progress. He continued to dig through the backpack, but he already knew that his efforts were in vain. Ben's face fell. He knew the answer before he asked, but he voiced his question, anyway.

"Did anyone bring a can opener?"

Badgy and Billy shrugged, each of them patting their pockets in the way friends do when you know that you're going to end up covering dinner this time. Ben sighed again, throwing up his hands in resignation. Just another incident in a seemingly endless string of bad luck. Ollie however, did not respond, his attention fixed somewhere in the middle distance. Ben's eyeline followed his friend's gaze until he, too, saw the object of Ollie's fixation. Standing there atop the hillcrest was the nightmare creature, the distorted monster. Ben knew it immediately—on the rare occasions on which he was afforded sleep, he had seen those nightmarish eyes too many times in his dreams. The same chill that he always got in the distorted creature's presence ran over his body.

There was no denying it any longer, the decaying creature was following Ben and his friends, watching over their every move. Ben's biggest question was why? He worried the answer was sinister. Unfortunately, the young hero would not have much time to ponder. Ollie's eyes were not, in fact, focused on their oinking observer but rather the throng of infected creatures coming toward them over the hill. Ben was already beginning to miss the relative comfort and safety of the Lucella Sewer System.

They had barely managed to catch their breath and they were already being set upon by a roving gang of the Infected. It was becoming clearer to Ben by the moment why the Entity's followers were more than happy to trade in their olfactory comfort for the safety of the indoors. Ben dug in Officer Doggy's backpack, rummaging around until his fingers closed around one of the tin bean cans. Tearing back his arm, Ben released the can, flinging the heavy container at the nearest infected creature. Ben's aim was honest and the can struck true, a creature nearly twice Ben's size stumbling to a dazed halt as the cylindrical metal container cracked against its massive skull. It was no junior varsity baseball tryout, but it would buy the quartet a much-needed ten seconds.

Ben turned back to Officer Doggy's backpack, withdrawing the canine law enforcement officer's trusty taser. The device charged up with the same dull whine as an old disposable camera, a flashing green light telling Ben that the device was ready for use. Billy and Badgy had already leapt into the fray, Billy fending off hostile creatures with his massive steel barbell while Badgy attempted to get clean shots with his crossbow. This core four had been adventuring together for so long at this point that they worked together as a unit. That was the beauty of teamwork, the fluidity of cooperation. A good team covered one another's weaknesses while complementing one another's strengths. Strength was not something that was in short supply while Billy was around. The bulky bovine pinned several of the infected creatures beneath his barbell, allowing Badgy to circle back around and load them up with the cure.

Almost instantly, their aggression lessened until they were practically cooing, each of them drifting off into a peaceful sleep. When they awoke, they would be confused and likely miles from home, but they would be safe.

No longer wielding the alligator's rusted pipe, Ollie had nothing to rely on in this fight but his wits. Luckily, for Ollie that was more than enough. His small frame made him a difficult target for the infected creatures, and like many children his age, he seemed to *never stop moving*. Just when one of the creatures thought that they had their paws on him, he was gone—or even stranger, somewhere else. No doubt it was this agility that had kept Ollie alive and well during his time in the wilds of Lucella. Ben was not as nimble as his friend, but he quickly learned that what he lacked in the ability to move quickly and easily, he more than made up for in the ability to discharge tens of thousands of volts of ionized electricity with the press of a button.

One of the infected creatures let out an undulating cry as the taser's two darts made contact with its flesh, electricity coursing through its body and temporarily incapacitating it. As if taking part in a choreographed stage play, Badgy flitted by moments later, unloading a singular cure dart into the creature's meaty rump. Ben wiped sweat from his brow with the hem of his shirt, adjusting his jacket around his shoulders as he surveyed the area for any more of the creatures. Ben turned to look back over the hillside, but just as Ben had predicted, their pallid pursuer had long since disappeared into the thick Lucella fog. Ben let out a loud sigh of exasperation as he picked up Officer Doggy's backpack and slung the sack back over his shoulders. The straps dug into his shoulders uncomfortably, but Ben had grown so accustomed to carrying this particular weight he felt almost bare without it. Ben had Ollie retrieve Agent Willow's map from his backpack, unfurling the rolled-up piece of paper on the dewy grass.

It took Ben a moment to track their progress through the sewers, but if his cartography skills were up to snuff, Ben and his friends had made their way beneath half of Lucella. Ben could not help but pump his fist in excitement. They were closer to their goal than ever, closer to ending all this—closer to getting back to normal. Glancing over at the sleeping frames of the creatures who had been out for blood just moments ago, Ben wondered if "normal" was something that Lucella could ever achieve again. He took a moment to gather his wits, using the glaring white moon overhead to orient himself according to the map. But that bright white light overhead was no moon. It took Ben's eyes a moment to adjust to the glare, but when they did, he was greeted by an illuminated sign bearing the image of a single grocery cart. Ben's heart skipped a beat and his stomach began to do backflips.

That explained why the infected creatures had seemingly been waiting for the four young heroes. These creatures were likely usually found wandering around the grocery store, but their hunger and curiosity had been piqued when they heard Ben, Billy, Badgy, and Ollie coming out of the sewer system. Ben wasted no time taking off down the hill toward the grocery store, his friends following close behind him. He pushed through the automatic double doors before they could whisk open ahead of him, his eyes going wide as they took in the grocery store's inventory. Unlike the grocery store nearest to The Safe Place, this location has not been purloined by hungry monsters.

Row after row of colorful containers filled with food lined the shelves, aisle after aisle of airtight jars

hermetically sealed to keep them fresh. A nearly crazed chuckle spilled from Ben's lips, seemingly contagious because before long the entire group was laughing. The quartet split up as they made their way down the aisles of the grocery store, shoving food into their bags and into their mouths. They were surely eating too much, too fast, but they would suffer their stomachaches later in silence, and they would be well worth it.

Ben barely managed to register the labels of the food he was eating before he was tearing it open and pouring it down his hungry gullet, safety seals snapping with a dull pop. An aisle over, Badgy was wrestling with several bags of chips—over and over Ben could hear the sound of air escaping a bag and the crunch of crisped potatoes against chisel-like incisors. Billy, too, must have been indulging his hunger as Ben heard the distinct sound of the bull's barbell hitting the ground. It was rare enough that the four of them got to enjoy a meal, even rarer a meal that was uninterrupted. Ollie disappeared to the frozen food section and returned moments later with ice cream that, outside of a faint hint of freezer burn, Ollie swore tasted just as good as he remembered. Badgy continued to move throughout the grocery store gorging himself on eggs and honey, apparent cornerstones of any healthy badger's diet. Ben doubted that a badger's diet called for them to drink honey directly from the bottle, but he also did not know enough about the average badger's food intake to argue the point.

The quartet stuffed their faces until they had eaten their fill, and then ate some more. When they were finally sated, they drank, each washing down their impromptu feast by passing Ben's water canteen to one another. Ben let out a sound of satisfaction as he wiped his mouth with the back of his hand and the back of his hand on the front of his pants. He could not remember the last time he had felt satisfied, let alone full.

Brushing various crumbs from his lap, Ben stood to his feet, making his way through the winding aisles of the grocery store and grabbing anything that he could fit into Officer Doggy's backpack. Perhaps most importantly, he swung by the hardware aisle. Wrenches, hammers, drills, and power tools had long since been cleared out of the inventory, and for reasons that were obvious. When it came down to an apocalypse, one could never be too prepared. Luckily, Ben was not currently in the market for home improvement. The tool that Ben sought was a bit more utilitarian in purpose, and as he made his way down the aisle, the metallic mechanical device caught his eye. Ben reached out for it, his hand clasping around a can opener as he pulled the device from the shelf and tossed it into Officer Doggy's backpack.

The cheeks on Ben's face were beginning to grow sore; he had not held a smile for more than a couple of moments in longer than he could recall. That unfamiliar feeling of satisfaction washed over Ben once again. If he was not careful, he might begin to get used to it. Ben circled back around to the front of the store and checked in on his friends. Besides what was sure to be an oncoming case of gas, they were fine.

Ben slumped over, holding his hand to his stomach, full for the first time in memory. It had been so long since he'd had a full stomach, he had almost forgotten how sleepy it made him. And when was the last time he had gotten a good night's sleep, anyway? Had it been the last time they had touched base at The Safe Place? Perhaps it had been the last time he had slept in his own bed. Maybe even before then. Ben's eyelids grew heavy and his body went limp as, even under the harsh fluorescent lights of the grocery store, Ben drifted off to sleep.

If he thought that a full stomach would make the difference in a restful night's sleep, Ben was woefully mistaken. His dreams were populated that night, as usual, by the haunting eyes of the decaying creature that seemed to follow them wherever they went. He tried to run, but the eyes cut him off at every turn, horrible floating orbs that appeared as if from nowhere. He tried to run, but his legs would not obey him. It was like he was not in control of his own body, a non-playable character in someone else's game. As if that were not bad enough, the Entity was still out there, floating somewhere between nightmare and reality. His ghoulish hands held Lucella in a vice grip, especially if the graffiti that littered the sewer system were any indication. The Eye of Insolence floated in the vast nothingness of Ben's subconscious, joining the ever-watchful eyes of the distorted monster. In Ben's dreams, his friends were not there to save him. He could not run, he could not hide—he had no recourse but to succumb to the horrors. The Entity's body materialized in front of Ben, a long gangly hand reaching out for the young hero, cold and clammy fingers wrapping around Ben's body as the Entity put him to his mouth and devoured him whole. Ben tried to scream, but no sound came out and he woke with a start.

Ø Ø Ø

The menacing off-color eyes of the Infected were not only limited to haunting Ben's dreams. As his eyelids fluttered open, the first thing he saw was the creature eye, yellowed and glassy, taking in his body as the creature sniffed him with a massive, snot-covered nose. Ben recoiled from the creature instinctively, his body curling up and away as he let out a startled yelp. It seemed that his voice worked better in the waking world than it did in his dreams, his nonplussed scream causing Badgy, Ollie, and Billy to wake with a jolt.

Ben was not sure how long the four of them had been asleep in that grocery store aisle, but it had apparently been long enough for a half-dozen infected creatures to make their way into the store. The creature closest to Ben had been sizing him up for an early morning snack when Ben had awoken from his nightmare, startling them both. Ben scrambled to his feet, just narrowly missing the sow's deadly gnashing jaws. Ben put as much distance as he could between himself and the chomping molars of the creature. In this case, that meant climbing the shelves of the dairy aisle. Officer Doggy's taser was tucked safely away in the backpack, which until a few moments ago, Ben had been using as a pillow. Ben swung the backpack at the creature as it reared back, once more trying to take a bite out of him. The others scrambled to their feet, frantically searching for their weapons through bleary, sleep-deprived eyes. It was a fight that the four of them had been in a hundred times over, but Ben was about to try something they had never done before.

Hopping down from the shelving unit, Ben turned tail and ran down the aisle. Past the illuminated rows of dairy products, past the checkout counters and cash register tills, straight out the front door. Ben had spent so much time over the last few months diving headfirst into these fights, he had forgotten that flight was a perfectly valid part of the natural fight-or-flight response. He did not owe any of these creatures a fight. Badgy, Ben, and Ollie seemed to take their cues from Ben, stowing their weapons and survival tools and following Ben out the door. Badgy stopped by the cash register on their way out, shoving fistfuls of tokens into his pockets. The automatic doors shot open for the quartet with a hushed whooshing noise and then behind them again as the monsters failed to give chase. It seemed that the infected creatures had been in the market for an easy meal and were too lethargic to give chase. For now, they would laze about the grocery store, feasting on anything that was not wrapped or sealed, waiting for the next poor unsuspecting soul to wander into their midst.

Ben's legs kept pumping, even as they carried him far, far away from the grocery store. It wasn't until Badgy, Billy, and Ollie stopped to catch their breath that Ben even realized just how far he had taken them. He rummaged around in Officer Doggy's backpack for his canteen, unscrewing the lid and pouring the water down his throat. Even when not facing a viral outbreak, it was important to stay hydrated. His breathing returned to normal as he retrieved the map from its special pocket in the rucksack and spread it out over a dry patch of dirt. He could almost hear Agent Willow yelling at him now, chiding him for not checking in periodically, and asking him just what was taking so long. He was so used to the wolf's admonishments, it was almost as if her voice was in his very ear, demanding that he answer her.

"Uhhh . . . you going to pick that up?" Ollie asked, pointing to the walkie-talkie hanging from Ben's hip. Commands blared sharply from the device, a tinny facsimile of Agent Willow's voice barking a harshly worded diatribe. The agent's voice had not been a figment of his imagination. He must have turned the communicator on by accident in the process of fleeing from the creatures at the grocery store. The concrete structure that housed the Lucella Sewer System would have most likely blocked any outgoing signal, and Ben had been too distracted by the thought of a meal to check in after that. Ben fumbled for the blocky, plastic device, uncoupling it from his belt loop and turning up the volume. He brought the device to his lips, and gritting his teeth and closing his eyes, he held down the transmission button, bracing himself for the full brunt of Willow's wrath.

"Hey, Agent Willow!" Ben sang almost sweetly into the handheld transceiver. The leader of The Silver Paw was less than sweet in her reply.

"What took you so long? You're reporting in late!" Willow growled from the other end of the walkie-talkie.

"Listen, Willow, we really were just about to get back to you. Nothing to report here, but we're definitely getting closer. We'll be in touch, over and out!" Ben released the transmission button and turned the machine off, ending the conversation as soon as possible. The agent's heart was in the right place, but she could be overbearing on her best days. Ben holstered the machine back at his hip and turned back to the map, tracing his fingers over their journey so far.

It was hard to believe just how far they had come, and he wasn't just talking about the distance they had traveled. Almost every location on this map told a story. Memories came flooding back to Ben as his eyes trailed over the unfurled piece of paper. The first time he had seen an infected creature was in the suburbs of Lucella. The search for gas at the police station had brought him to the gallery. Ben smiled as he remembered the first time he had met Badgy and Billy, and their subsequent adventure at the mall. Ben remembered the icy chill in the air as they had sailed to Doveport in search of components for the cure. With the map laid out in front of them, it was a small wonder that they had made it this far. How many times had this journey almost been cut short? Officer Doggy had disappeared into the night in the forests outside the city without so much as a trace. Ben still could not fathom what could have happened to the canine officer of the law, but he found it best not to dwell on it. The symbol that marked the Metro station only brought back memories of Sally Squirrel. They had not spent much time together; Sally had stayed behind to fight against a swarm of infected creatures, buying Ben enough time to escape on the train. Sally's sacrifice had allowed him to eventually find Ollie, which was all he had set out to do.

It seemed only natural to look back at how things had begun, now that they were coming to the end. It took Ben a moment to orient himself, but once he did, it was a piece of cake to locate their position on Willow's map. If the map was to be believed, their destination was an old laboratory and hospital on the outskirts of Lucella. Their distorted friend was not the only one with eyes all over Lucella. Agent Willow's Silver Paw agents had intelligence that there was a concentration of infected creatures gathered at the hospital, the likes of which they had never seen. It was a frightening claim; Ben knew those agents—he knew what they had seen. Though what had piqued Ben's interest was the mention of a helicopter. The only person on the island who Ben had ever heard of owning a helicopter was the elusive Mr. P. Ben would have gone into more detail were there more detail to be had, but for now, by Ben's best estimate, the hospital they sought was just over the hills.

Ben stood and adjusted Officer Doggy's pack on his back. The police officer's old walkie-talkie hung from his belt and his taser was at the ready. From the corner of his eye, he could see Billy hefting his steel barbell over his shoulder and Badgy counting out his remaining cure vials as he loaded them into his crossbow. It was best to check their inventory now—as they were entering what seemed to be the final level— after this, there would be no turning back.

It did not take very long for The Silver Paw's information to be proven correct. As they came over the crest of the hill, they were greeted by hundreds—if not thousands—of infected creatures. The Silver Paw agents were right, it was like nothing that Ben had ever seen before. The creatures stumbled over one another like crabs trying to escape a pot, too overwhelmed by their sheer number to do anything but stumble into and over one another. And in the distance—Ben could not believe his eyes—a helicopter.

If the army of infected creatures was not enough to tell Ben they were heading in the right direction, the helicopter surely was. It was no surprise that at the center of the catastrophe, there was a billionaire. Ben and his friends had fought their way across two whole islands at this point, but it was worth noting how often they'd had numbers on their side. Ben thought back to their mission to retrieve part of the cure from their old school building. They had awakened one of the infected creatures from its slumber and of course it had given chase, as these creatures were wont to do. It had taken the combined ingenuity of all four of the young heroes to stop that one single creature. They had failed in the tunnels beneath Doveport. If it had not been for a stroke of luck and a burst of quick think-ing, this quartet would almost certainly be operating as a trio. Still, as Ben looked to his right and his left, friends still flanked him on both sides. A feeling of pride swelled within him and for a moment he felt as though—even if the odds were a million to one—they were in his favor.

"So, Ben. What's the plan?" Ollie asked, stepping up to join Ben in looking over the hillside. Ben was quiet for a moment, racking his brain for anything even remotely resembling a coherent plan of action. He found nothing. He had heard it said that the best laid plans often went awry, and it was an idiom that he had seen put into action more times than he cared to. Ben's eyes did not waver from the swarm of infected creatures milling about at the base of the lab as he announced to his friends the closest he could muster to a plan.

"Survive," Ben stated firmly as he began his trudge down the hill.

Ollie was the first to join Ben, picking up his pace to match step with his friend. Billy followed not far behind, the sound of bullish footsteps falling in step behind Ollie and Ben. A steady stream of muttered complaints meant that Badgy was not far behind them. The unit moved as one, ducking behind boulders and hiding behind hills as they made their way down the slope to the face of the laboratory.

It took them what seemed to be the better part of the day to make their way to the entrance. Each time they made headway, they were forced to retreat into hiding by another wave of the infected creatures passing by. Two or three of the creatures were no matter; it was nothing they had not handled before. These creatures, however seemed to rove in much larger groups, and Ben had come too far to end up as an appetizer plate for a hungry ghoul. The quartet ducked behind an oversized rock as another group of the creatures lumbered by. A half-dozen pairs of mismatched eyes scanned the area where Ben and his friends lay frozen in wait. Ben held his breath, convinced that even the minute rise and fall of his chest could be the straw that broke the camel's back and got them discovered. He dared not peek around the corner to see if they had been found out, yet the anticipation was slowly killing him.

After what felt like an eternity, Ben saw the creatures move on—one, two, three, four, five sets of shuffling footsteps receding into the distance. One creature remained behind, though; Ben could see the shadow it cast on the grass and hear the deep guttural sounds it made as it breathed through its mucus-ridden mouth. Ben swallowed hard, a dry lump rising in his throat, the pit falling out of his stomach as he waited to be discovered. Inhaling deeply, Badgy held his breath as he pulled out the crossbow and loaded an empty vial into the pull-back mechanism.

Badgy closed one eye and aimed toward the other side of the path, squeezing his finger around the trigger. The empty vial went soaring, the projectile launched by the powerful spring-loaded device, and it landed across the way with a tinkle and a crash, the empty vial shattering upon impact. The noise caused the creature to turn with a start, turning away from the four heroes to search for the source of the sound. Ben's heart began to race; he was almost certain he could feel the organ banging against his rib cage as if demanding to be let out. With the creature momentarily distracted, they abandoned their hiding spot, dashing through the darkness to the next safe space.

They repeated the process for hours: find a place to hide, wait, run. Find a place to hide, wait, run. It was a nerve-racking pattern to be sure, but it was keeping them alive and therefore was better than the alternative. The closer they got to the base of the lab, the thicker the fog seemed to grow until the white vapor seemingly enveloped the entire building. It was not long before the only way to avoid the bloodthirsty creatures patrolling the base was to look for their eyes floating in the dense vapor and to listen for their low, heavy grunts. By the time the four young adventurers had reached the front gate of the lab, a full moon had risen over the island of Lucella and hung itself lazily in the sky—somehow managing to just barely shine through the thick layer of gathering fog. With assistance from Officer Doggy's flashlight, Ben could just barely make out the numbers on the keypad to the lab. Another memory flashed across Ben's mind: The last time he had needed to break into a mysterious laboratory, the notes he had found inside had led them on the journey that would lead to the cure.

While Ben appreciated a full-circle moment, he had no intention of repeating history by deciphering this key code combination. Raising Officer Doggy's taser to the keypad, Ben held down the capacitor until the light on the device turned green, indicating a full charge. Introducing the taser's charge to the keypad, the machine fizzled and flashed, a shower of sparks exploding forth from the blackened keypad. A small spiral of black smoke coiled from the box and snaked into the air and the door unlatched and popped ever so slightly open. Billy and Ben opened the door the rest of the way, grabbing the door by its edge and sliding it open, and then closed it behind them. It was another lesson they had learned from their first time raiding a secret lab: It was always best to keep your exits covered. Ben flipped a light switch and immediately wished he hadn't. He had been expecting another horde of the Infected, but as the overhead lights chugged on one by one, what they revealed was so much worse.

There were dozens of the infected creatures here, yes, but none of them were awake. Kept afloat in giant glass tubes, all the creatures seemed to be in a state of suspended animation. Notes were scrawled on charts attached to clipboards sitting next to the glass cylinders. If you had asked Ben an hour ago if there was anything worse than the horrid red eyes of these creatures, he would have been hard-pressed to answer.

But standing in the laboratory with these lifeless eyes staring at him from behind glass, filled to the brim with some mysterious, sickly green fluid—Ben would agree that this was somehow worse. He tried to read the charts beneath, but they were far beyond his level of understanding. Though Ben was certain he didn't need a medical degree to know what he was looking at. These were test subjects. Test subjects for what exactly, Ben wasn't sure, though he was certain that answers were incoming, whether he liked them or not.

## THUD!

A loud banging noise on the outside of the door startled the quartet. The chorus of inarticulate grunts that accompanied the sound let Ben know that the infected creatures knew they were here. Ben's eye darted upward. Of course, they had been drawn to the lab when Ben had turned on the lights. As long as the infected creatures stayed outside, Ben and his friends had nothing to worry about. Ben consulted the laboratory's directory. The lab was connected to the hospital via an elevator. Whatever was going on in that hospital was the key to all this. Badgy leaned in to examine one of the glass cylinders more closely. The creature that floated inside was hooked up to all kinds of monitors and machines. Badgy tapped on the glass absentmindedly, a tiny **tink tink** sound echoing throughout the lab as Badgy's nail made contact with the glass.

The creature inside opened its eye, focusing an angry red pupil on Badgy. Bubbles erupted from its mouth as it roared in the tank, pressing its cloven hooves against the glass. It closed its eyes just as quickly, the machines beeping rapidly. Badgy leapt back in surprise, stumbling backward into the laboratory's keypad. The door whisked back open, several dozen pairs of hands grabbing Badgy and pulling him back through the door. Billy screamed, grabbing his barbell set and leaping into action, plowing through the creatures as he attempted to grab Badgy back from them. Soon, even Billy succumbed to the sheer number of them, both he and Badgy being swept away into the swarm. Ben moved to go after them, but Ollie held him back, grabbing him by the hem of his jacket.

"We have to go!" Ollie shouted over the rumble of footsteps, the infected creatures trampling over one another as they came pouring in through the door. Ollie was right, though Ben couldn't help but scan the horde for signs of Badgy and Billy as Ollie pulled him away. The duo broke into a run, bolting down the laboratory hall as quickly as their legs would carry them. Behind them, a veritable wave of the creatures crushed everything they came into contact with, leaving only destruction and the smell of old bacon in their wake. Ollie pressed the elevator call button frantically, the red digital display counting down the floors before it reached the ground level. Ollie pressed the button again, as if jamming it repeatedly would suddenly make the elevator car appear. The elevator arrived with a pleasant **ding!,** and Ben and Ollie leapt inside before the doors had even finished opening. Ollie pressed the CLOSE DOOR button desperately, and the elevator doors gave a frustrated whine as they whisked shut. Through the elevator shaft, Ben could hear the tell-tale sound of the creatures ramming their heads against the elevator doors.

Music played gently over the speakers as Ben and Ollie rode the elevator in silence. What could they say to each other that had not already been said? The elevator continued its journey to the hospital floor, a cheery ding! as they passed each level. Seconds passed, turning into long minutes before the elevator doors finally slid open, greeting Ben and Ollie with the unmistakable, sanitized smell of hospital air.

They were in the right place. The elevator doors closed behind them, taking the light and music with them instantly. The hallway was plunged into darkness, the only light now coming from a room at the end of the hall. From the end of the hall, Ben could see the silhouette of a single person. He crept toward the room, Ollie following him in turn. Placing a hand on the doorknob, he took a deep breath, giving Ollie a solemn nod. Ollie returned the nod and Ben steeled himself for whatever may come next as he turned the doorknob and entered the room.

It took Ben's eyes a moment to adjust to the harsh overhead lights of the hospital room. Charts covered the walls, almost papering the room from floor to ceiling. In the corner, a machine beeped steadily, a series of thick wires attaching the machine to a bed. In the bed, a woman lay unconscious, hooked into the machine by a series of tubes. A chessboard sat in the middle of the room, a game abandoned seemingly mid-match. The silhouette remained in the corner of the room, shrouded in shadow. "Mr. P, I presume?" Ben asked, moving his hands to his belt. The shadowy figure rose from its seat, turning to face the boys. An orange-red eye floated in the darkness, giving way to the distorted creature that had been stalking their every move. The creature stepped into the light, somehow looking even more horrible than before. The creature had decayed even further since their last meeting and it stumbled as it walked.

"Sit . . ." The creature moaned in its horrible guttural voice, gesturing to a seat in the middle of the room.

"But . . . but you can't be Mr. P!" Ben stammered, trying to put it all together. The helicopter, the walkie-talkie . . . Ben's mind was reeling.

"He's not Mr. P . . ." came another voice from the corner as a man stepped into the light. "I am."

Mr. P was a purple sweet potato of a man. A small and thick black mustache swallowed up a button nose sitting beneath beady black eyes. Mr. P wore a black suit and pants, with a matching fedora adorned with a white flower. He had shoved brown socks into black shoes and had a red tie hung crisply around his neck. If this were truly the wealthiest man in Lucella, he was certainly dressed the part.

"We don't get many visitors," Mr. P stated casually as if he were discussing the day's weather. "Do share how you came upon us."

"Long story," spat Ben curtly.

"Yeah," added Ollie. "It would probably take three decent-sized novels to tell it all properly. Maybe four, but I'm not greedy."

"Please. Sit," Mr. P offered, gesturing to the empty seat. "I'm sure you'll want to hear my story, and he won't ask again." As if to emphasize Mr. P's point,

the distorted creature in the corner grunted loudly.

Ben took the seat in the middle of the room. Mr. P must have caught Ben's eyes trailing over the chessboard.

"Do you play?" asked Mr. P, a spark of excitement

gleaming behind those beady little eyes of his. It was becoming clear that the decaying creature had been Mr. P's only chess companion for a long time. "The game of kings and the king of games. It goes all the way back to India in the sixth—"

"We know what chess is," Ollie interrupted. "It's a way for writers to make a character seem smart without doing the legwork. Now what *exactly* is going on here?"

Mr. P took a deep breath before he began and gestured to the woman in the bed, still hooked up to all the machinery.

"This is Mrs. P." Ben's eyes flickered across the room to the woman, really taking her in for the first time. "I was developing a cure to the sickness my wife, Mrs. P, had. I put all my time and money into saving her. I even rushed the doctors to test the supposed cure. The doctors kept telling me the cure was unstable, but I didn't listen and I needed volunteers."

As Mr. P continued on with his story, Ben's jaw dropped and his eyes went wide. The distorted creature before him wasn't a monster at all—he was a test subject. Of course someone like Mr. P would be keeping tabs on the happenings of Lucella, sending the decayed creature out to keep watch and report back. "Then came the kind Piggy family . . ." continued Mr. P. "They wanted to help."

A shiver ran down Ben's spine as he thought about how much experimentation Mr. P had done in the name of saving his wife. The creatures floating in liquid downstairs must have been just the beginning; the proof of his failure was currently banging their heads against the elevator doors. An entire swarm of infected creatures—an entire island of monsters—all because of one man's hubris.

"The initial results were significant. The test subjects became stronger. I was overjoyed, so I gave the cure to Mrs. P immediately. Substance-128 we called it. She was getting better until we heard news that the test subjects had started becoming hostile." That was an understatement. Mr. P's cure was turning people into infected monsters, highly contagious creatures of low brain power and immense hunger.

"I thought it had nothing to do with my cure, but eventually Mrs. P became aggressive, too. The last time I saw her, she had been lost to the sickness. I wanted to stop her but didn't have the heart to, so I let her go. I tried again to make cures. Then you came along. We found signs of the Infection within you, but you were still alive."

Ollie's eyes met Ben's. It was true. Back in Doveport, he had thought he had been scratched, but when nothing came of it, he pushed the thought from his mind. He had almost forgotten the incident entirely until now.

"I tried to do more research, the hospital we were at was raided, and Sally and I were separated. That's why I tasked you with rescuing her. Tell me, where is Sally Squirrel now?" Ben looked to the floor, unable to answer. All the people he had lost over the last several months, and he was finally face-to-face with the man responsible.

"I gave my wife another rushed cure, thinking it would save her. I realized what I had done and brought her here." Mr. P stood with a drawn-out sigh. "There you have it. That is my selfish, sorrowful story."

No one spoke for a moment until Ollie broke the silence. "Cool story, you're still going away for a long time."

"Oh, my dear boy . . ." Mr. P smiled as he pressed a button on the wall, calling for the elevator. The doors opened with a familiar ding! Ben could hear the creatures from the lab, grunting and growling, waiting for their next chance at a meal. A sea of red eyes advanced into the lab, each one of them forced into this life by the man in front of them. "Even if you were leaving this place alive . . . you're children. Who's going to believe you?"

That seemed as good a time as any. Ben stood from the seat, his hands moving to his belt once more. "You get all of that, Agent?" Ben asked.

# KRSHH!

Static clicked on the other line of Ben's walkie-talkie, fastened to his belt. "Loud and clear" came Agent Willow's response from the communicator.

# CRASH!

Glass shattered as Silver Paw Agents descended from the ceiling, surrounding Mr. P and the distorted creature. Agent after agent flooded into the room, weapons drawn as they secured the area, neutralizing creature after creature effortlessly. One of the infected creatures lunged to bite Ben, finding its teeth instead wrapped around the wrong end of a stainless-steel barbell. Billy smiled down at Ben, pulling him into a bull hug—which was much like a bear hug but with obvious, bovine differences. Superior weapons and tactics brought the fight to an end quickly in favor of The Silver Paw. Bringing up the rear, following half a dozen Silver Paw agents, was Willow herself. She marched directly up to Mr. P, a handful of agents already forcing him to his knees. Willow presented a pair of silver handcuffs.

"Mr. P . . . by the authority of The Silver Paw, you're under arrest for crimes against Lucella." The Silver Paw agents handcuffed Mr. P and pulled him to his feet.

"You . . . heard everything?" Mr. P asked Willow. "You were listening . . . the whole time?" Ben nodded. He knew the quickest way to ensure that Willow followed up with him was to hang up on her.

"What can I say?" Ollie chimed in. "We're professionals."

The Silver Paw agents grabbed Mr. P by the elbows and began to lead him out of the room, but Ben stopped them with an extended arm. He had one more question for the man. "I'm sorry, but . . . didn't you learn

something here? That you can't do whatever you want? That actions have consequences?"

Mr. P raised his head slightly to meet Ben's gaze. "My dear boy . . . When you're rich and powerful, you only learn the lessons that you choose to. We'll be back." Ben quirked a brow. *We?*

The Silver Paw agents led Mr. P out of the room and made arrangements to carefully transport his wife to The Safe Place. Ben gave Mr. P one last look over his shoulder, and he could have sworn he saw the Eye of Insolence looking back at him. Or was it just his imagination? The distorted, decaying creature was being tended to by several Silver Paw agents. The dinging of the elevator was much less ominous on the way down, though Ben was surprised he could hear anything at all over the sounds of Badgy cursing loudly as Silver Paw agents loaded him into an ambulance. He had taken quite the beating, but after a quick patch up, he would be no worse for wear.

Badgy gave a thumbs-up as they loaded him into the vehicle. Ben, Billy, Willow, and Ollie walked outside, the sun shining through the fog, dispersing the mist and illuminating a clear morning sky for the first time that Ben could remember. He looked at his friends and smiled. There had once been an island called Lucella. Far past Doveport and somewhere south of the North Sea. Its outer edges were sprinkled with long beaches and stretches of picturesque mountains that led to a salting of dense forests. In the middle of the island was a city, a sprawling metropolis bustling with life. On a normal day, thousands of people went about their daily lives—tending to their gardens and watching one another's yard for the occasional monster.

On a normal day, crossing guards waved children across the street to school, and neighbors greeted one another cheerily as they passed on the streets. On a normal day, the sun hung low over the island, casting a lazy glow across the city. The island of Lucella was due for a normal day.

## About the Author and Illustrator

**Terrance Crawford** is a humor and pop culture writer from Detroit, Michigan, who lives in New York, New York. At the time of printing, he still has not received his Hogwarts letter.

**Dan Widdowson** is a children's illustrator from Loughborough, England. He graduated from the Arts University Bournemouth in 2014 and has been working on children's illustration projects with The Bright Agency ever since. With a keen interest in storytelling and narrative, Dan is working toward bringing his own picture books to life in the near future.